Southcrop Forest

Southcrop Forest

Lorne Rothman

iUniverse, Inc.
New York Bloomington Shanghai

Southcrop Forest

iUniverse books may be ordered through booksellers or by contacting:

iUniverse
1663 Liberty Drive
Bloomington, IN 47403
www.iuniverse.com
1-800-Authors (1-800-288-4677)

Because of the dynamic nature of the Internet, any Web addresses
or links contained in this book may have changed
since publication and may no longer be valid.

This is a work of fiction. All of the characters, names, incidents,
organizations, and dialogue in this novel are either the products of the
author's imagination or are used fictitiously.

ISBN: 978-0-595-49588-7 (pbk)
ISBN: 978-0-595-61163-8 (ebk)

Library of Congress Control Number: 2009925100

Printed in the United States of America

For Carolyn,
Arielle and Quinn,
and the last great oaks along the Iroquois Bluff.

Contents

Prologue

Budburst

"Wake up! Time to wake up! The days are long. The sun is warm," cried voices from all around.

Auja roused herself from slumber, let out a yawn and stretched her limbs. Her stretching stretched on until the new moon grew full. She sprouted a pale green halo.

☼

Food at last. Come on little Fur, it's time to feast. Fur is what he called himself. He was pleased with the name. It was not the first, but it seemed to fit on account of the fur that coated him. He had tried others—like 'Oak'. There were oaks all around and he felt a part of them somehow. But he had no leaves or bark. Nor was he stuck in the ground. So 'Oak' was out.

Fur was no tree. He was a tree dweller—born way up high on a south facing branch with plenty of sun. And today was a fine day for sun basking. The sky was clear blue and that bright ball of fire warmed the air. But he could not laze about any longer. He was starving and had to find green food.

His first foray would not be easy. It was the starting part that troubled him most. He lay huddled on a twig, clutching it tight, too scared to move. The great expanse of forest and sky made his fur stand up on end and quiver. But his hunger won out. *First food, then fear.* He gathered himself up and crawled clumsily toward the scent of fresh leaves.

Part I:
Auja Meets the Runes

Hardwood Forest

Auja's acute senses returned in full as she basked in the morning spring sun. Her branches and twigs tingled all over as the warmth drew life back to her outermost edges. From the forest depths, she heard the haunting song of a hermit thrush. Her fresh leaves bristled as the sound drifted by. Two chickadees burst on the scene, tickling her as they played acrobat in her lower branches.

Wildflowers were sprinkled all around her. She inhaled their sweet scents, and thanked the gardener trees who had worked so hard for this moment. The bright forest floor was now fully flushed with red and white trillium droplets and pink pools of spring beauty.

Auja was a red oak, neither all female nor male, but both.[1] Her ragged crown of lustrous green hung lank over slate-grey boughs. If very lucky she would grow up to be a grand northern hardwood. Tall and strong, she would carve a place in the sky and show the sun her full splendour. But that day was a long ways off. She had just begun her fruiting years and her bark was hardly roughed in.

Auja lived on the edge of a glade and was surrounded by her kind. From her vantage, a large granite outcrop, she could see a lowland bog. The sharp silhouettes of spruce and fir gave a hint of what lay far to the north in the realm of Dark Forest.[2] Beyond the bog lay the Oak River,[3] marking the borders of her Southcrop Forest.

A small creek swollen with spring rain burbled down a gentle, rocky slope to the south. It was a perfect spot for animal watching. The snowshoe hares lived in the willow thicket by its banks. The fisher[4] and bobcat came there to drink and hunt. The black-winged damselflies would soon emerge to flutter in flocks above the waters.

The trees were silent this morning as they soaked in the warmth. The dry chit chatter had faded. The tedious debates of dark winter were through. Auja gazed around her small glade. It was good to see friends and family and feel Southcrop come alive once again. Spring was a time of such promise.

Then she remembered. All of a sudden, her branches drooped and her leaves lost their sheen as she bore the full weight of the tragedy anew. Southcrop Forest had lost another farm.

Farms

In the beginning sun gave life to the earth. Then the earth grew trees to watch over life and make the world a better place for it to thrive. And to aid with this charge, the earth gave trees their treasured farms, so all could stand together as one.

Quite the tall tale, likely sprouted by teetering elders long ago. But they had the gist of it. Like hewmen[5] without machines, trees were lost without their farms—the source of their power and vitality. Farms were the core of the forest web that enabled tree culture to flourish for nearly four hundred million years. Without farms there would be no speech paths, no communication, no hellos to ones' friends from afar.

Auja had been told of golden days before her time. Farm and forest ranged so widely, you could hear a voice across the continent and swear it came from someone you could touch with your own shadow. Then the hewmen came ashore and changed everything.

These days the world of trees was so much smaller. Auja could not speak to others beyond the ever shrinking borders of Southcrop Forest. And as the trees disappeared, so too did their farms. Last fall, another was destroyed. The hewmen came and trampled it, then smothered it with false-rock.[6] Only two remained in Southcrop and not for much longer. Both were within reach of the machines now gathering for fresh kill.

What would happen after all the farms were gone? She could hardly bear to think. The forest web would fail, the trees would grow weak and sick, and tree voices would fade away to whispers. Auja's leaves quivered at the thought. Trees were not meant to stand alone. The solitude would drive her mad and she would find an early death without the farms' life-force to sustain her.

Auja did not fear only for herself but for friends and family and all trees in this land. The Southcrop way had flourished here ever since the last of the Big Ice.[7] All great and small things that gave life meaning—the art and science, fable and lore—would soon be forgotten. It would take hundreds of thousands of years to recover. A new age of loneliness was upon them.

What could be worse than to lose everything you ever had? Maybe to lose something just found that could have bettered life for all. These were no ordinary farms. Ten years ago, they bore magical fruit that allowed trees to do much more than hear each other's voices. With this new found treasure, trees could share their sensations. Sights, sounds, smells and even feelings of every tree in the web were now within reach of all. Southcrop Vision—their greatest discovery—would die along with the farms. No one beyond this forest would ever know.

Auja felt utterly helpless. She was a trivial tree—so young and green. Nothing she could ever do would change anything. Best to drift back to slumber and find some pleasant dreams. She would never get away with such laziness. There was too much work to be done.

Crawlers

Despite the impending doom, trees were doing what they always did this time of year—counting. It was the spring census. Time to survey the animals and plants.

"What's the point?" Auja asked her neighbour oak. "We should relax and savour what soon will be gone."

"Point is—it's the tree way," her friend said. "We've got to keep track of our world and all its changes. Stop distracting me. I'll have to start over."

True enough. The counts had been useful in the past. But so much had changed in the last fifty years it was hard for trees to make sense of it all. What good were measures and tallies now? Their way of life was about to end.

The wise elders had spoken. The census would continue as usual. But why? Maybe they were only trying to keep everyone calm. There was a secret plan and all would soon be called to action.

Action? What could trees do against hewmen and their biting machines? No, the trees were doing what came most naturally—burying their leafy crowns in the sky and pretending all was well.

Auja could not fight it. Best to start counting. She spotted some crawlers. These were the forest dwelling tent caterpillars,[8] and they loved to eat oak leaves. She knew them well. Insects and oak trees shared a long history.

She thought of that bit of verse from the song of life. *Tent caterpillars are a great wonder. Every decade or so, they rise up as one to smother the forests and strip the trees bare. The wandering hoards of fuzzy blue carve grey skeletons in the green.*

The words sounded cute and harmless, but Auja knew full well what they meant. There were twice as many crawlers in her branches as last year. And the more she had, the more she would suffer. Even now, so early in their season, they made her itch all over as they scraped her leaves.

At least they were easy to count. Tent caterpillars grow up together in colonies of hundreds, so they were simple to find. "One—two—three—four—it's the counting season and there's bound to be more," Auja chanted. "Twenty-three colonies so far! What about you, oak friend?"

"Fifteen. Lucky me," replied her neighbour.

"Make that twenty-four," Auja reported as she felt a fresh itch from a large and vigorous group working away at her topmost branches. "What have we here?" she added as she had a closer look. The crawlers in this colony were almost through their second stage.[9] Their mother must have been very clever, leaving them plenty of yolk for the long winter.

Auja stopped her counting and watched the caterpillars for a long while. Then she dangled one of her leaves in front of them to make them stir. Finally she stroked their hairy backs. That got their attention as several stood up on their hind legs and swung their tiny heads.

"What are you doing there, Auja? Playing with the creepy crawlers again?" asked neighbour oak.

"No, no—only taking a break," she replied. She was known for her strange attachments to crawlers and felt embarrassed. But there was no helping it—she was fond of them. Sometimes she even felt sad for their harsh and fleeting lives. Only the most able and lucky ones would survive all their crawling stages, and then the big change,[10] to greet on the wing and leave eggs for next year. They would then promptly die, never to see their own young.

And there was something intriguing about this colony. It was so big and lively. It was made of over two hundred and fifty brothers and sisters. As she watched, one caterpillar growing tired of shoving for scant food crawled off in search of a tasty new leaf. It found one close by and came back to show the others and bring them along.

Auja knew all the tent caterpillar signals and cues. They spun silk trails and doused them with chemicals to entice each other because there was strength and warmth and safety in numbers. They were still too small to survive on their own. By the end of this spring, branch and bole would be shrouded in silk. It would make her bark glisten on bright, dew-drenched mornings long after the last caterpillar was gone.

Auja watched as a new line of crawlers crawled between old leaf and new. It looked like a long winding limb reaching out for food. She imagined the colony was one creature with one will, rather than hundreds of brothers and sisters. She played this 'many are one' game with the ants and bees as well and could spend days pretending.

But this time was different. These crawlers moved in harmony. There was a rhythm to the swelling of their bodies as they walked, and their feet moved in perfect unison. Her toy picture of one-ness looked real this time. It was remarkable, extraordinary—too extraordinary. Auja's suspicion was aroused. "Hey, oak, what do you think of this colony?" she called to her friend.

"Still dilly-dallying, I see. What about it?" neighbour oak replied.

"Oh, nothing, nothing I guess," said Auja. But it was more than nothing. It was something—something strange. She did not want to draw any more attention, else the teasing would surely follow. Others less friendly than neighbour oak might not be so kind. She could already imagine the taunts. *What now, Wandering Oak? Making special friends with a blight? Or maybe you're being lazy—wandering off to avoid the work of spring count!*

Wandering Oak was her proper name but it was often used in a disparaging way. Why should anyone care if her mind wandered? How could she be interested in too many things? Focus makes a tree stiff and dull. She preferred a rich life brimming with varied endeavours.

Auja spotted a tiny creature flying towards the caterpillar colony from above. It looked awkward in the air, beating its wings furiously to stay afloat. She was a mother rogue wasp[11]—a deadly beast—looking for a crawler. With a touch of the tail, she would lay her spawn upon an unlucky victim before flying away. The poor crawler would slowly be eaten alive by the young wasp left behind.

That is what Auja expected. But something else happened instead. The colony put up a fight! All the crawlers, together at once, pulled themselves into a tight circle. It reminded her of stories about muskoxen that lived beyond the trees in Big White.[12] They would huddle up with their soft parts in and their horny heads out to ward off their foe.

Crawlers had no horns, but their heads were smooth and hard. The colony turned itself into a hard-headed ring, and then—by piling crawlers one upon the other—a black shiny dome. The muskoxen never managed that.

The wasp lunged wildly from one side, then another and above, trying to find a way through to soft bodies. It bounced off each time and soon gave up for good.

What's going on? Not possible, thought Auja. Tent caterpillars were not supposed to behave this way. In fact, she had never heard of any insect doing such a thing.

Maybe she should tell someone? But did it really happen? By now the colony had settled back down to eating and looked quite normal. Fear of ridicule made her doubt her senses. Best to forget it and go back to work. And so she did until dusk. But the thought of that strange colony beset her again when she stopped for her evening's rest. It made her sleep fitful as it crept around the edges of her mind.

Predators

Next morning Auja was disturbed from her slumber by a panicking hare dashing in full flight through the glade. And right behind it, flying way too low at break-neck speed, was a goshawk.[13] The race ended with a lunge, cries of pain, then silence. Hare was dead. Goshawk had food. No need to get excited. Bird chases mammal—predator eats prey—plants like Auja had other concerns. She was more interested in the leaf eaters.

It was not only tent caterpillars that feasted on Auja this season. There were the lace bugs, redhumps and floaters,[14] the borers, pruners, girdlers and gall makers, and the shredders and skeletonizers, for starters. Auja had to count each and every one.

Her train of thought was broken by a sharp, sudden cry. *Who or what was that?* she wondered. The voice had come from within her crown. She searched through leaf and branch but found nothing. Then her little pet project, that strange crawler colony, caught her attention. Most of the caterpillars were feeding together near the base of a leaf while on a nearby twig, a spined soldier bug[15] had already struck and was having its meal.

The bug was tan coloured with a shield-shaped body and spurs on its shoulders that made it look menacing. And to a young tent caterpillar, it was. Especially the one it had harpooned and sucked dry. The crawler was hanging limp on the bug's long pointed beak.

There was nothing too out of the ordinary here. *Must have been day-dreaming*, Auja thought.

Emergence

By mid-afternoon that big colony was feeding again. Auja had been watching it as it crawled to a new site, higher in her canopy. Tent caterpillars always went up.

"Why did you climb so high little crawlers? You'll run out of tree up there," she said.

"I know, I know. That's why I'll have to grow wings someday," came a faint reply.

"What … the … what did you say?!" Auja exclaimed. She felt a sudden shiver run under her bark. It started at the base of her trunk and spread out to every branch and twig in her body.

"Wings, I said wings! If you trees grew all the way up, I wouldn't need wings," the voice replied.

"Up … up to what?" Auja asked without thinking.

"The sun. It's where I came from and I have to get back—so I can make more crawlers. It takes two moths and the sun to do that, don't you know?"

Talking crawlers? Auja was not day dreaming after all. She was struck by a memory from her earliest years. *I know what you are.* The old legend was true. These were Runes. They had returned. "You can talk!" she said, addressing the colony.

"Yes, and so can you!"

"Of course I can. I'm a tree. But you? The whole idea is preposterous!" she said. "Who's the special crawler that speaks?" she asked.

"There's no special one. We're the one. We're all one together," the colony replied.

"But I only hear one voice," said Auja.

"I've only got one. I'm the colony. The colony is me. I'm we. We're me. Isn't that the way it's supposed to be?"

"No, not the way. Not at all," she replied.

Auja meanwhile pulled together all the pieces of the legend she could recall from her sapling days. There had been a magical Gathering of trees and people one thousand years ago by the eastern sea. The tent caterpillars had been there too, a nuisance as usual. Soon after the Gathering in the very same place, strange crawlers emerged that could speak to the trees. But they died from a terrible plague.

That was all Auja could remember. She had always thought the legend was about talking caterpillars—each with its own little voice. No one ever said anything about talking *colonies*. There was never a mention of sentient beings emerging like magic from the insect hordes.

"Why not the way?" asked the colony. "Aren't you also made up of smaller living parts?"

Auja had to think hard about this one. "Well now, that's very different. Yes I am. But I'm one organism. My parts act together. They're cells, not crawlers, and they can't live alone."

"My parts too. So what if they're crawlers? They can't live alone. At least not yet," the colony replied.

"No. That's not the same. You can't be. I'm a tree. I'm highly evolved—part of a great and ancient civilization that has watched over this planet throughout the long ages. You're only a bunch of insects. You can't be aware! You … you … Oh, bother." Her words tailed off in confusion. She had got what she had been calling for in her whimsical way—a response—but now she was having trouble coping with it.

Yet there was no denying this colony of crawlers was talking to her. And it spoke with a single voice. It was a single creature. It was one from many. What a discovery!

"What should I call you?" asked Auja, wanting to keep it talking.

"Fur."

"Why Fur?"

"Because I'm furry."

"What fur? Only the mammals wear fur."[16]

"What's a mammal?"

"You know—beaver and bat, martin and moose, squirrel and shrew."

"Say what?"

"Forget it. Fur it is for you," Auja said. It was a poor creature—knowing so little of the world—but a creature it appeared to be nonetheless. Maybe, just maybe, it could help them in their plight? It was meek and small and slow (it was a tent caterpillar colony after all), but at least it could move, and it seemed to understand the trees. She knew she could not keep this a secret.

Auja tried to contact the elders, but they were too busy and none would listen. She tried her more senior neighbours. But they had no time for her. "Well, you've outdone yourself this time, Wandering Oak. Go back to the count; there's much work to be done," was the only response she got.

Here was Fur speaking out for all to hear, but no one would take any notice. Auja would not be denied. She took matters into her own leaves and roots and used them to send the crawlers' voice drifting through the forest web. Surely someone would reply.

It was the elder Guide Oak who finally did. At one hundred and thirty years, the Guide was not really that old. She had joined the elders because of her wisdom and good sense rather than age.

Guide Oak seemed fond of Auja, often giving her time and attention usually reserved for more important trees. "What have you found, young Auja?" she asked.

"A great treasure," Auja replied. "I've got Runes in my branches!"

"Well, have you now?" There was something strangely calm about Guide Oak's voice, as if talking insects were an everyday occurrence. "I've heard your strange friend. It is no tree. Let me speak to it."

"Yes. Yes, of course," Auja said. Finally someone believed her.

The colony was nearing the end of its feed. Already a line was forming as the crawlers began to march away from their half-eaten leaf.

"Hey there, Fur. There's someone who wants to meet you. Do you mind saying hi to Guide Oak?"

"Hello there," said Fur. "Where are you? I can't see you."

"Never mind. I am far away but I have questions that need answers. Listen carefully," said Guide Oak.

"Sure," Fur replied.

"Who are you, little one?" asked the oak.

"I'm Fur."

"How did you come to this place, Fur?"

"I don't know."

"Where have your kind been all these centuries—hiding deep within some island forest?"

"I don't know."

"Did your parents and grandparents also have your gift?"

"What gift?"

"You talk to the trees."

"The other crawlers don't?" Little Fur's voice squeaked the question while his crawlers shuffled about and tickled the young bark of Auja's branches.

"No," replied Guide Oak.

The tickling stopped suddenly. Little Fur was now very still. "I don't know anything about my parents or theirs. I've never met them. It's not possible for our kind. We hatch in spring and die in summer. Only baby crawlers sleeping snug in their eggs can cross the long cold." [17]

"All right then," said the Guide. "There's much work to be done. Good day."

Strange, thought Auja. Guide Oak had seemed quite satisfied, though Fur's answers to her questions had not been very illuminating. The elder had not sounded surprised by little Fur at all. She was certainly not bursting with excitement. No matter. Auja had done her part. The word was out and it would spread. She knew what would happen next. A Gathering would be called.

"Hey, oak tree!" Fur shouted.

"What?" Auja replied.

"What do I call you?"

"Most call me Wandering Oak."

"Wandering? That's a weird name. You've got no legs and you're stuck in the ground," said the colony.

"It really has more to do with … with … well, no matter. My friends call me Auja."

"Owwja, Ajaaa, Auja.[18] That's weird too and hard to say."

"I know. It came from strange creatures from a faraway land. My mother gave it to me. She told me that nothing in life is for certain. And that's what makes life worth living. So she named me Auja—Auja for good luck."

"I could sure use some good luck right now. What about that nasty bug? Is it gone?" Fur asked.

"For now. But there will be more and more. Life will only get harder from here on out," replied Auja.

"Yeah, I get it. Maybe I've never heard of your mammals, but I know my worst enemies—and I know that more of my crawlers will die. The cold and wet have already killed. And if I lose too many more, I'll never live my dream."

"You dream?" asked Auja.

"Sure. I dream one day I'll grow wings and fly to the sun. Like I said, that's where I came from and I've got to get back. Maybe you can help me get there. Please tell me about this place, and you, Auja oak. I don't think I've much time."

You're right about that, Auja thought. "I'm your host," she said, addressing the colony. "Surely you know us oaks well. We've been together through the ages. This place is called Southcrop. It's a land of rock and lake, scraped by the motions of water and ice."

"Why Southcrop?" Fur asked.

"We live on a southern outcrop of the big rock," Auja replied. "The granite beneath my roots is part of a colossal plateau—the ancient bedrock of the continent.[19] More than ten thousand summers ago this was a frozen place. But the trees returned as the earth warmed and the ice melted. The hardy voyagers, spruce and tamarack, poplar and birch, were first to arrive. Next came pine and maple, and finally we oak, bringing up the rear, pushing to the northern extent of our ranges.[20] And now here we dwell together in our isolation. We are bound by man-trails, farmlands and sprawl, by Windy Bay,[21] the Oak River banks, and the shores of Ouentironk[22] and Lake Attigouatan."[23]

Several of Fur's crawlers started to crawl away from the group as Auja spoke. Was she losing her audience already?

"Well, thanks for that," replied Fur, "I didn't catch it all, but it sounded quite thorough. Talking trees indeed! How do you know so much?"

"I've learned through the word of others. We speak through our roots and the soil surrounds and sometimes through our leaves where the canopy is unbroken. We speak to our neighbours and they to theirs too and on our words travel, or so it used to be.

"There once was a time not so long ago when our speech paths ran true all the way down to the southern tips of the earth. But the forests are in decline and our lines have been cut. And there's worse to come yet." Auja's leaves drooped as she was reminded once again—the best of times for trees on this earth were over. "Maybe you can help us! You can go places we can't!" she added, excitement building within her.

Auja was cut short by sharp creaks from the boughs of her neighbours. The other trees were listening. "Wandering Oak, Wandering Oak, you had best be more quiet and careful," whispered many trees together.

Auja knew she was saying too much. If the elders did have plans for this creature, it was not Auja's place to reveal them.

"I hear other voices too—lots of them!" said Fur. "Who are they? Are they coming to ask me questions too?"

"No, no more questions for now. Only trees' chatter," Auja replied. "Guide Oak and I are not the only ones. All of us trees can speak—whether broadleaved or evergreen. We're all friends here."

"The needle bearers too?" asked Fur.

"Sure. Each has something to offer. We've all got a part to play. See that white pine over there?"

"Yuck! Sharp leaves and no food," Fur said. "What good is it?"

"That tree is my friend," Auja replied. "And she helps me to see during the long dark winters."

"See? Where are your eyes?" asked Fur.

"Well, now they're all around you. Our leaves are our eyes. We have thousands of them that feed on the light. That's what makes hardwood vision so extraordinary. Imagine our acuity and range of view!

"Each spring, we leaf out and watch the warm season unfold into days of long light and rich green. Then, when the sunlight weakens and the air grows cold, our eyes fall away and we slowly go blind. The blazing forest fades to brown and white before the long darkness arrives."

A dozen crawlers reared up together on their hind legs, pointed their heads skyward, and began to sway.

Is this creature pointing? Auja wondered.

"What's that then, eh, bright eyes?" said little Fur.

He is pointing, Auja thought. She looked up and saw a black speck slowly circling in the sky. "Yes, good eye—remarkable in fact! It's a turkey vulture, a large scavenger."

"If I could fly like that, I'd head right for the sun. Imagine the view from up there!" said Fur.

"How can you see that?" Auja asked. "It's so far."

"I see it fine. Remember, I'm the whole colony. I too have eyes all around."

Gathering

Guide Oak had spread the news of Auja's discovery. For two days, Auja listened to the rush of voices and leaf rustlings that ripped through the forest like brisk breezes of spring. No one mocked her anymore. Trees spoke with wonder and awe.

It was Gathering day and a fine day it was, as the damp cold had given way to bright sun. Auja was ready. She was not the only one. She could feel tension in the air.

Fur noticed something was up. "What's going on? What's with all the whispering?" he asked.

"We're having a meeting today," Auja replied. Fur had made his way up to the top of Auja's crown by now. His many feet prickled her and she could smell the scent of cut leaves as Fur chomped away at her green tips.

"About what?" Fur asked.

"An important discovery."

"Can I come?"

"No, not this time. I'll tell you about it after. It'll be really boring. Think I'm a big talker? You haven't heard anything yet. The talking could go on for days."

Gatherings were reserved for the most important occasions. They were mostly about fires and logging and their dwindling farms, so they were sad and serious affairs. And given recent events, this one would be the most ominous. The thought of little Fur lifted Auja's spirits as she settled herself for the lengthy proceedings. Fur could help them to send word beyond Southcrop—and maybe more!

A Gathering. Auja found the choice of words quite funny and chuckled to herself. She had watched many animals gather over the years, but they did it on foot or wing. It was a much trickier affair for her kind. But then trees had been talking to each other for so very long, they knew how best to bring voices together. There was no need to move. They had their forest web through which they could speak—though maybe not for much longer.

"Welcome all to our Gathering," Guide Oak called out. The Guide was balanced and fair and had a knack for debate and so was the usual choice to lead.

A smattering of 'hails' and 'greetings' from various trees about Southcrop tapped Auja roots.

"It will most likely be our last," Guide Oak continued. "We all know Southcrop Forest stands alone! The man-trails have grown wider. Our voices cannot breach their false-rock. All our attempts to reach the outside world have failed.

"And now we must bravely face our final end," Guide Oak continued. "Our last two farms will soon be gone. Then we will be nothing more than scattered, lonely trees waiting for our roots to shrivel and die. We cannot save ourselves. But must our greatest discovery die with us? Must all our memories be lost forever?"

The questions hung in the air. The forest grew silent and sullen. Even the warbling 'chur-lee' of the finch in Auja's branches stopped short. Birds were simple creatures, but when the forest web surged with emotion, even they could not escape its effects.

"We will not let our Southcrop way be forgotten!" said Guide Oak. "We will not let our Southcrop Vision perish—not without a fight! We have one last hope. Auja has discovered Runes!"

"But there's only one," muttered Auja quietly to herself. It was loud enough.

"Only one? A single crawler? What good is that?" cried a muddle of voices from every direction. There seemed to be some confusion about little Fur. Messages had a funny way of jumbling when passing from tree to tree.

Guide Oak's voice rose up to restore the order. "Yes, it is true. There is only one. But the one is many. The Rune creature is a colony that thinks and speaks as a single being. It can help us. We can send it to one of our remaining farms to gather our treasure and then carry it beyond the borders of our land."

So the elders did have a plan for Fur, Auja thought. *Excellent.*

"But we must hurry," said Guide Oak in a rushed voice. "This colony will only be with us a very short while. When the crawlers reach their fifth stage and scatter for their big change, the Rune creature will die. And our farms will not survive much longer. The hewmen machines are poised to strike. So now we must decide. Which way do we send the Runes? To Rock Edge Farm in the south or Riverside in the north?"

Elder Beech was the first to make her case. Beech was a large, symmetrical tree, with lovely buttressed roots. Her light grey bark grew tight and smooth. Her coarse-toothed oval leaves were pale and fresh, though they would soon turn a dark green later in the warm season.

Beech lived in the southernmost reaches of Southcrop, where the granite was covered over with rich soil and man-farms. She preferred mild winters and long summers. It was not hard to predict where her arguments would lead.

"I say we go by way of Rock Edge Farm. I would dearly like to send greetings to the south. Remember the days when our lines ran clear to the shores of Lake Yenresh?[24] It was not so long ago that tulip, walnut and sassafras numbered amongst our friends. Let us send Southcrop to these grand deciduous trees."

A gruff and booming voice called out in reply. It was remarkably low and thunderous. "You should not let fond memories cloud your reason. The shores of that lake are no longer wild." It was the biggest voice in the land and it belonged to the Sentinel. The Sentinel was a white pine. Auja could see her off in the distance. Her magnificent silhouette jutted up to the sky. She towered over the forest—an emergent who could see further than any other tree. Her full spreading branches leaned this way and that and ended in billowing clouds of long needles.

"It is not only Lake Yenresh that I speak of," the beech replied, "but all the south, where many fine trees stand. There have been routes down that way in the near past.

"And this has nothing to do with fond memories," the beech continued. "The strength of treekind comes from our diversity. How else will we adapt to the change that is to come? We should all look to the rich southern forests. Let us send the Runes south-west to cross the big man-trail. On the other side, around the beaches and the bay there may still be lines to the limestone escarpment and the millennial cedar.[25] From there our lines should be clear at least down to Big Falls."[26]

Auja knew of these famous cedars and had heard their voices in her youth. Imagine living for one thousand years. Most trees would count themselves lucky if they made it past one century these days.

These ancient trees were revered by all. It was obvious the beech was using them to strengthen her argument. It worked. Forest voices rose in a crescendo of applause.

"The crawler Runes are nomadic by nature. But it is too far," Sentinel Pine replied. "They will not be able to reach the man-trail[27] before their big change. Even if they could, who's to say the southern trees stand together? Do they have their farms? Is their forest web intact?

"The south is so crowded with men," the pine continued. "Surely their sprawl has turned forest to false-rock by now. And what if our words did reach south to Lake Yenresh? Then what? We join another fragment bound by the Great Lakes and the River Divide."[28]

"Then the Runes must go north." It was the ethereal voice of Herald Aspen from the near-shore of Oak River. She had a look and feel of grace and light. Her slender, green-white trunk glowed whether in sun or moonshine, while her bright round leaves shimmered in the slightest of breezes. Aspen had turned one century this season. She was a very old tree for her kind.

Auja admired the aspen. They were free-spirited pioneers. They ranged more widely than any other tree, even up to the tree line where few hardwoods dared to grow. They knew all the tree dialects. Many were fluent readers of Bird Sign.[29] They were quick to grow and had wide, spreading roots. They were the stewards of the speech paths that ran through the forest web.

"The only hope for us now lies to the far north in the fertile crescent of Dark Forest. It is the last great forest on earth," said Herald Aspen.

"What? Did you say Dark Forest?" said Elder Beech. "Hah! It is a barren land with a harsh frozen climate, short growing seasons and poor soils. The trees are all stunted. What's so fertile about that, you fleeting little tree?"

Beech had a point. But insults were not helpful. Sure, the aspen did not grow big or live long, but the Herald was wise well beyond her years. Auja could hear the anger in the beech's voice. And, thanks to the wonders of Southcrop Vision, could even feel the heat in her words.

"Dark Forest is our final refuge," replied the aspen. "It sits atop our globe and reaches out to all. It is the core of our communication network. From there the speech paths run clear in every direction. If you want to send word across the continent it must go by way of the dark green.

"And all that passes through also remains," Herald Aspen continued. "It is there that our memories linger and the tree way may yet thrive. As the plague of hewmen continues to spread, it will become our final home. If Dark Forest falls, then so too will treekind. We will enter the darkest age of our earth—an age of loneliness and forgetting. I say we must join the fertile crescent of Dark Forest. All is not lost if we look to the north!"

Auja's hope rose with these final words. She knew Herald Aspen was right. There was no other way. She could not contain herself. "Yes! What a grand idea!" Auja cried out. "Southcrop Vision will reach the true north, and spread along the fertile crescent. It'll flow along the upper shore of Kitchi-gami,[30] then south and east through the continental forests and the tired, old mountains to the tropical lands." Her words spilled out. There was no holding back. "It'll drift westward and along the jagged peaks to who knows where or how far. Maybe it can reach the other end of the earth. Imagine it! A new, world-wide forest web—bringing all trees together as one!"

"Hurrah, here, here!" a few cheered.

"Young fool," most others jeered.

So much for Auja's excitement. Those last words burned her like a late frost at budburst. It was unusual for a youngster to speak out. Auja had found little Fur. But this did not give her the right to stir emotion with wild flights of fancy. She resolved to keep quiet for the rest of the meeting.

Auja believed whole-heartedly in the northern route. She wondered why Guide Oak wasted so much time letting others have their say. Enough talking—it was time for doing. It was time to send Fur on his way.

But then Auja was also swayed by something much closer to home. In her younger days, she had taken an interest in the planets and stars. And that interest lingered. While false-light[31] now dimmed much of her night sky, just north beyond the Oak River there was a place of pure darkness. The Southcrop trees now called it Deep Sky.[32] There the views of space would be grand. What better place to send their gift?

The deep, throaty voice of Elder White Spruce was next to be heard. Spruce was a large and impressive tree, rivalling even the white pine with her presence. She had a thick, conical crown of dark green tinged with blue, growing from a long and slender, scaly brown trunk. Spruce ranged widely across the continent but felt most at home in Dark Forest.

"I agree. We must send Southcrop to Dark Forest. But north across Oak River is not the way. Let us send the Runes to Riverside Farm and then across the Big East Trail above Windy Bay. From there our lines should be clear to the highlands and the Southern

Envoy of dark green.[33] What better place to send our gift and our greetings—to the hill-top sugar maples and the lake shore emerald groves of fir, cedar, hemlock and spruce."

Guide Oak replied, "Yes, a good suggestion. There are fine woods there. But how will the Runes cross the Big East Trail? It is so very wide and never free of machines. Maybe there are too many men that way."

"What do the rest of you think?" asked the oak. "Come now, everyone must have their say."

A weak and broken voice crept through the Gathering. "Why go anywhere at all?" She was Ancient Sugar Maple, the oldest tree in Southcrop. And her age was showing, to be sure. She had a hole in the middle of her trunk. You could see right through it. And one side of her bled golden amber from the rot. She was a favourite haunt of the birds, and even now a fine red-headed woodpecker was hammering away at her trunk. "Dark Forest is too far and the south choked with false-rock! There will be broken lines and fragments whichever way you choose. All the farms must be long dead.

"And who's to say these crawlers will help," the maple continued. "Why would they? Talk is easy. But action? Ha! We no longer have the power to change the world. Our dominion over this planet is through. We must accept our lot and savour the twilight years of tree-kind."

The forest went quiet. The sun slipped behind a cloud and the shadows crept in. Guide Oak broke the maple's spell with her fiery reply. "Do nothing? Yes, that would be so easy. You go ahead, tired maple, and lie down to rest. But we will not ignore our good fortune. Our Wandering Oak, our little Auja, will find a way. She will turn these Runes to our cause!"

Whoa, hold on there, thought Auja. She was all for action. She was an impatient tree. But what could *she* do? "I'm too young," she said. "It's too important. Sounds like an elder's job."

"You found the Runes," said Guide Oak.

"His name's Fur," Auja added.

"All right, you found Fur. He dwells in your crown. You must watch over him, but only for a little while. There is crawler plague nearby, and it is spreading. He will die if he stays here. You must convince him to leave and help with our quest. Will you do this for us, Auja?"

Darned crawlers, why'd Fur's mother have to lay Fur on me? Auja should never have come to this Gathering. She wished there was somewhere she could hide.

"Yes," she finally replied. What else could she say?

With that matter settled, the meeting changed course. There were so many details! The talking would go on and on. All trees would have their say. Auja listed them off to herself—*cedar and pine, tamarack and spruce, hemlock and fir; oak, maple, basswood and beech; serviceberry, ash, mountain ash and elm; birch, poplar, hawthorn and hop-hornbeam; dogwood, cherry, sumac and willow ...*

There were many crawler questions. What foods do they eat, how much do they need, how far can they walk in one day? How long before they turn into moths? What beasts would hunt them on the way? And these were no ordinary crawlers. Fur was a legendary creature. The historians would soon be scouring the archives for thousand-year-old memories of Runes. Auja had no patience for details. She had a job to do. Best to get started.

☼

The Gathering ended three days later and well after dark. Little Fur had since gone to his bed—a mat of soft silk spun by his crawlers. Auja listened as Guide Oak gave her summary of the plan. "The Rune creature will go to Deep Sky," she said. "It will follow the Rapids Trail.[34] When the trail veers westward, it will stay its course and journey north through the forest to Riverside Farm. There it will cross Oak River along the silver lines.

"The journey may take more than a full lunar cycle,"[35] the elder oak continued. "We must guide the Rune creature and keep it alive. We must feed it our most vital information to carry to Deep Sky. This is our last chance. Let us give it our best!"

Ancient Sugar Maple tried a final objection. "How will the creature remember all that we tell it?"

"Legend says Runes are carriers," replied Guide Oak. "As the creature feeds, our thoughts will become part of it. We can only hope the old stories are true."

Guide Oak turned her attention to Auja. "Well, my young friend, it all begins with you. Please take care. We will all be watching. Better hurry now. Time is running out! You must send your little Fur on its way."

A New Stage

'Better hurry?' *'Time's running out?'* The elders spend days prattling away over minutia, and when they finally run out of wind it is Auja who must make haste.

Things would work differently now that Auja was in control. She was a quick and clear thinker. Her part was easy. All she need do was start little Fur on his journey.

To that end, Auja had spent three days chatting with Fur and learning his ways. She found that Fur could only hear her speak while he was eating her leaves. But eating is what he did most mornings, afternoons and evenings and sometimes in between, so the two had plenty of time to get acquainted.

Auja was surprised to discover she enjoyed Fur's company. He was a curious creature, always asking the most basic questions. Yet he had a burning hunger to learn about all sorts of things. And he wanted to know everything straight away. It was as if he understood how fleeting his life was.

Fur was especially interested in the sun. He seemed obsessed with it. This was a nice coincidence. So was Auja. She loved the sun—for the most obvious reasons—she was a tree and fed on its light. But there was more. Over the years that fireball had led her on a voyage of discovery. She learned how it drove the weather in Southcrop and the climate around the globe, how it moved water and air, and carved the landscape,[36] how it set patterns in motion and maintained the earth's order, how it sustained all life on her planet. Finally, here was someone with the same curiosity; someone with whom she would share her sun thoughts.

But little Fur was starting from scratch. "Where does the sun go every night? Will it always come back?" he asked after the Gathering's end as the sun went down. His voice quivered while his crawlers quaked.

Was he actually afraid the sun might set for good? "Doesn't go anywhere, as far as we're concerned," replied Auja. "It's us that moves."

"How's that? You're stuck fast in the ground," said Fur.

"Not only you and me—all of us—everything—the whole of the earth. It's round and spins full circle around itself once a day," she replied.

Auja spent a long while convincing him of these basic facts,[37] after which he appeared relieved—which was a relief to Auja too, since it put an end to Fur's trembling crawlers, whose tiny hairs prickled her until her leaves went numb.

But then more questions followed. "What about the hot and cold?" Fur asked.

That led to a chat about seasons, the earth's axis of rotation and its orbit around the sun.

That prompted other questions from Auja's simple but eager companion. "How do you know the earth spins round the sun? How can the earth tilt if it's round? Does it lean to one side? What's it leaning on, eh?"

And on and on and on ... Thankfully, Fur could not eat forever, and once his crawler guts were full the questions stopped. Fur retreated to his bed of silk for the night.

There were more pressing things to talk about than universal placement of stars and planets. What of the quest? Auja had better hurry. Time was not on her side. The skin of Fur's crawlers looked worn and tight. Auja figured little Fur would soon have to moult to his third stage.

She was right. Next morning she watched as one of Fur's largest crawlers reared up on its hind legs as if to get an early peek at the rising sun. Its body then began to heave and swell. A rip in its skin appeared near its head and grew, exposing fresh colours beneath. Others crawlers did the same. One by one all their skins burst open.

The faded lines along their brown bodies now shone bright blue. The row of spots along their backs glowed clear white. It was over in time for late breakfast. The crawlers marched in single file out to Auja's green.

"Feeling better? You look dazzling," said Auja as Fur began to eat. Auja did not mention how funny the crawlers looked with their oversized heads and loose skins.

"Thank you," Fur replied. "I've more room to grow. These leaves taste better than ever."

"Good, eat well," said Auja. She braced herself to ask the question that burned inside. "Little Fur, I need you to do something for us."

"Which us this time? The whole of the earth?" he replied.

"No. Southcrop Forest and all trees in fact—and now that you mention it—yes, the whole of the earth."

"Sounds important."

"It is—very!"

"How can I help?"

"We need you to carry something for us to Deep Sky."

"What 'something'?"

"A message or two and a special gift. We'll tell you all about it later."

"Where's Deep Sky?"

"Far to the north across the Oak River."

"Far? How far's far? You mean like over to that ash tree?" Little Fur pointed to the edge of the glade using two of his crawlers that stood up on their back legs.

"No, much farther—many days journey for you," said Auja.

"I don't like the sounds of that. Why don't you send it yourself?"

"We can't reach it. But you can. You crawl."

"I've got everything I need—bright sun and good food. No thanks. I'm not going anywhere," Fur said.

"But you're our only hope!" cried Auja.

"Maybe I can help from here?"

"No. If you stay you'll be no better than a tree. It's the moving part of helping that's most important to us."

"But … but I'm frightened. I'm too little. It looks too big," said little Fur. His voice began to quake.

"What's too big?"

"All of it. Everything that starts where you end. I can't go out there. I'm sorry."

Blasted crawlers, thought Auja. By now the whole colony had started to quiver again. And she had only just recovered feeling in her leaves from Fur's last bout of fright. Maybe this was not going to be so easy. She had better get some help.

Southcrop Vision

Auja sent out a call through the forest web for Guide Oak, who seemed none too please by the disturbance. The Guide lived at the other end of Southcrop Forest. But her reply, once sent, returned in a flash (a flash being about one million times faster than a crow could fly from the elder to Auja—even with a favourable tailwind).

"What do you want?!" asked the Guide.

"I'm sorry to bother you. I'm having a bit of trouble moving Fur."

"Why?"

"He's scared."

"If the creature is too frightened to leave, then make it even more frightened to stay," said the Guide. "Good day, Wandering Oak. You must get rid of those crawlers now!"

☼

It was Auja's turn to quiver. Her rustling leaves and branches startled Fur from his meal.

"Whoa there! Is that the wind or you? I nearly fell off," said Fur.

"Sorry about that." Auja regained her composure and started right in.

"Listen Fur. You can't stay here. It's too dangerous."

"What do you mean? I've done fine here, thanks to your tasty leaves and sunny patches. I'm at my third stage and have over two hundred and fifty crawlers. My chances are looking pretty good," said Fur.

"The good times won't last. Have you seen the other crawlers?" Auja asked.

"Sure, their silk trails are everywhere. I haven't followed any yet but I will soon enough. I'd like to find some company."

"That would not be wise. You crawlers have done well the past few seasons and have multiplied too quickly. There are too many and you'll soon begin to decline. The wasps and flies are gathering. They're waiting to infect you with their young. It's already started. Remember those rogue wasps?" asked Auja.

"Sure, but I fought them off with no trouble," said Fur.

"Yes, that was impressive, I must admit. Some got through though, I'm sure. Can you feel the doomed amongst you? Alien creatures will burst from your crawler bodies. Rogue wasps are only the beginning."

Auja's words seemed to have no effect. Little Fur kept munching away. She took a different tack. "And then there's the virus."

"What virus?" Fur asked.

Surely Fur knew of the virus. He had said he knew all his enemies. Auja tried again. "The crawler plague."[38]

Fur's crawlers froze in their tracks as she uttered these words. There was no shaking this time, but all their hairs rose up stiff and straight. "Have you seen it?" asked Fur in a shaky voice. He did know of plague and seemed to fear it. Auja could not blame him. Nothing was more dangerous and gruesome.

Auja did not want to press further. But she had to get him to leave. She felt awful but continued. "Yes, there are many sick colonies in the forest, and the cool, wet spring has not helped. New reports are arriving daily. Your numbers are sufficient, the conditions just right. There will be a terrible outbreak.[39] It will spread like a wildfire. The cycle of your lives will be broken and your energy stolen. You'll all die here."

"Stop! Please, enough! What does it matter if I stay or go? My enemies are everywhere," said Fur.

"No, not so. This is one of the worst places to be. The birds, wasps and flies will gather. Plague will run rampant. If you want to live, you'd do best to leave. And we can help. We can warn you of dangers ahead—maybe even show you."

"Show me how?"

"Using our special gift, our Southcrop Vision."

"What's that?"

Hmm … Why not now? Auja wondered. *Good a time as any to give it a try.* Fur could hear Auja speak but could he see the world through her leafy green eyes?

"Hey. Where'd you go?" asked little Fur.

It was as if Auja had shut down. But she hadn't—not really. She was only trying to concentrate. Not that what she was doing was so hard. Normally it came second nature. But this time was different, of course. This time she was trying to share across the kingdoms of life—from plant to animal—tree to insect. It was simply absurd.

But so was little Fur, and yet there he was, chomping away at her, asking her questions—so who was to say it had to end there? Maybe Auja could push this further. Time to try. She began to send Southcrop images to her fuzzy companion. She dredged them from her deepest root tips and sent them surging up and out to her leaves—and into the many mouths of Fur.

Auja focused her sights on the colony, so that Fur might see himself from all angles at once. There was really nothing quite like this tree view. It was sure to get his attention. A reverse panorama would describe it best—with eyes all around looking in at the middle.

Then she went in search of dangers. And for the hoards of tent caterpillars about Auja's glade, there were plenty to find. She saw a stealthy soldier bug waiting to pounce and pierce and a sly rogue wasp hunting on the wing. She found a fly laying eggs on oak leaves, put there to be eaten by crawlers. She gathered these images and sent them to Fur.

Next Auja called upon her friends and used their leaves too so that she might see and show things beyond her own crown. She found a pair of cuckoo birds. Though most birds did not eat hairy crawlers, cuckoos loved them and could devour whole colonies.

And finally she found a young victim of plague, far away on an aspen tree. It looked more like a blotch than a crawler; its body had already dissolved into goo. But the purple stain of the disease was unmistakable. Auja watched little Fur for a reaction. There was none.

"Do you see anything unusual?" Auja asked.

"No, what's to see?" Fur replied.

"No matter," said Auja. Maybe it was not possible to share Southcrop Vision with her strange companion. Auja continued with her plea. "If you leave here we'll help you to stay alive. If you stay you'll die. That would be such a terrible loss for all. Will you help us?"

Fur did not respond. He walked away from the last of his meal. The conversation was over. Auja would have to try again—and soon.

☼

The next morning was overcast and grey. The sky hung close to the ground. "Nothing like a cloudy day to dampen the spirit," said Auja, as Fur gathered around a breakfast leaf.

Fur was slow to speak and seemed shaken. "I had a really weird dream last night."

"Do tell," said Auja.

"It was as if … as if … I was seeing through different eyes."

"What did you see?" Auja asked, the excitement building inside her. She figured the Southcrop images she had sent to Fur had finally reached him.

"I saw myself from above and below and from every side, and all at once. Then I started to float through leaves and branches. I could see and feel everything around me. I watched as other crawlers marched in search of food while enemies hunted them down. I tried to warn them but they couldn't hear. And there was the ugliest creature. It was a hairy dark fly with huge brown eyes. She was sneaking about, up to no good, I know."

"A swift fly[40]—up to no good indeed," said Auja. "Her eggs are deadly traps. If a crawler eats one, it will die slowly and give rise to a writhing white maggot. And there are more nasty flies to come. You may know your enemies, but do you know all their devious ways? I can teach you. We trees can help."

"Wait, the dream didn't end there," Fur interrupted. "I glided along from one tree to the next. I saw a big brown bird with a grey and white tail. Its beak was curved and its eyes had red rings. It flew slowly from one tree to the next. Then I heard a 'cu-cu-cu' as another appeared."

"Black-billed cuckoos," said Auja. "They'll gorge themselves on crawler flesh this season. And they are building a nest nearby."

"I saw my enemies in that dream. They'll try to kill me," said Fur. Auja felt a tickle as Fur's crawlers trembled. "But it was wonderful too."

"Why's that?" Auja asked.

"The seeing and ... the flying! I thought maybe I was a flock of moths at first. But I couldn't find my wings. I couldn't find any of me. Where'd my bodies go? What happened to me last night?" Many of Fur's crawlers paced back and forth as he spoke.

"Easy Fur, I took you on that journey. You shared my senses. I told you tree vision is extraordinary. Our leaves are really the most remarkable organs."

"Wow! Yes they are. So I ... I borrowed your leaves?"

"Yes," replied Auja.

"How?"

"Southcrop Vision, that's how!"

"But what about the floating and gliding? You can't do that. You're stuck in the ground."

"You saw through the leaves of other trees as well."

"How's that possible?"

"Like I said, Southcrop Vision! We trees have been talking ever since there were forests. But now we can do more. We send pictures—not only of what we see, but all that we feel!" Auja's leaf-tips tingled with the thrill of it.

"And I can feel them too!" said Fur.

"Yes, that's excellent. Odd that it took so long, but no matter. You'll get better at it, I'm sure. If you have limits, we've not reached them yet." Auja was delighted. Little Fur could *see*! Was it enough to get him moving?

"Did you notice the plague?" asked Auja.

Fur's caterpillars pulled in to a tight circle and faced out, as if they could somehow ward off the microscopic enemy with their hard heads. "Yes, I think so," he replied. "Did that crawler die on you? Are your leaves polluted?" he asked in a whisper.

There was no plague on Auja yet. She knew this as did everyone else. Trees could see into many worlds within worlds within worlds and were keenly aware of all life forms,[41] no matter how minute.

Auja knew full well that every tree in Southcrop was listening. She knew what they expected her to do—lie! She was supposed to say, "Yes, you're surrounded by plague. Now run along before you're infected." And why should she not, for the greater good? Had not Guide Oak told her to scare Fur away? She had no other choice. It would be so easy to trick this simple creature and send it fleeing in terror.

Or maybe not. Alas, Auja had never quite mastered the art of deception. She was an honest tree to the core and the truth flowed out from crushed leaf to crawlers who swallowed it whole before she could dam it inside.

"No, I'm clean. You're safe," she replied, "but only for now," she added realizing too late that she had given up her chance. The elders were right. She was a young fool. She would suffer dearly for her candour.

"Well then, I'm better off here than out there," said Fur. "I've had my fill for this morning. Thanks again for that excellent dream trip. See you at next feed," he said. He marched off to his resting pad and lay there stretched out in a brief burst of sun. The sunshine was short lived. The clouds let loose a hard rain.

Auja was not left alone to sulk in silence on this wet and dreary day. Southcrop Vision would not allow that escape. From all around and throughout the forest web, she was overwhelmed by the sensations of others. First anger and regret, then a terrible anxiety, and finally despair battered her leaves in gusts and surged up through her roots as the canopy air grew stormy and the soils flooded over with the passion.

Finally by evening Auja was chased to fitful sleep by all the emotion the trees of Southcrop heaped upon her. Later that night she dreamed she pulled up from the earth, turned her roots to feet and strode across the land. With one giant stretch she stepped clear across Oak River and let her acorns fall to the ground beneath Deep Sky. There they burst wide open and showered soil with magic seed from every farm that ever adorned Southcrop Forest.

No such luck, Auja thought as she awoke the next morning. She had no acorns yet this year, and once grown they were sure to be quite ordinary. And as for the walking, well, that was preposterous. Tree movements were limited to:

1. Leaf lifting, drooping, curling and shaking.

2. Twig jiggling.

3. Bough bending.

4. Growing (but that was slower).

5. Migration (as when oaks returned to Southcrop after the Big Ice. That was really slow and hardly counted since they were seeds doing the moving, not trees).

6. Transplanting (as when hewmen dug up trees and put them elsewhere).

Sadly, 'ripping root from rock and roaming free' had never made the list. Trees, as Fur put it, were stuck fast in the ground. And that is why the trees, despite their wondrous powers, had so much hope resting on a heap of little crawlers. And that is why the forest came down so hard upon Auja when she had refused to lie—simply to rid herself of Fur.

Auja noticed Fur stirring. The rain had finally ended and he was getting up. He must be hungry. Except for one brief afternoon feed, he had gone without food all the day before. She expected him to race out into the warm light of sun and gorge himself on some breakfast leaves. But Fur did not rush anywhere. He looked slow and sluggish and barely nibbled on the meagre leafy crumbs by his resting pad.

"Good morning, Fur. How are you doing today?" asked Auja.

"Oh, what's the point," he replied.

"Of what?"

"Eating, crawling, doing anything. We're all doomed. What a sad and dreary forest. What a hopeless world," he replied. His voice sounded distant and cold.

"What's wrong with you?" Auja asked.

"All's lost. It's your fault." Fur shook three crawlers at Auja's trunk. "You couldn't do one simple thing for Southcrop, could you?"

"What are you talking about?" Auja said. It was as if little Fur had joined the rest of the trees to scold her.

"You should've lied! You should have forced it out!"

"What it?" Auja asked.

"It … the Rune creature … me!"

Now Auja understood. The trees were speaking through Fur. The angst of Southcrop Forest that had battered Auja yesterday had passed through her leaves and on to little Fur. All it took was his afternoon snack, and wham, it must have hit him later while he slept. This creature was now fully part of the forest web.

Extraordinary, Auja thought. "Hey come on. Snap out of it, Fur," she pleaded.

"What's happening to me?" Fur seemed to be returning to his senses. "Something very sad and heavy has taken hold of me! What is it?"

"Us," said Auja, "all of Southcrop Forest. Now you understand our plight. You can feel it, can't you?"

"Yes," Fur replied. "Oh, please make it stop, please!" Little Fur was now squealing, while his crawlers wriggled and writhed.

"I can't. Only you can," said Auja.

"How? Tell me."

"By leaving this place and carrying our gift across Oak River to Deep Sky."

"What gift?"

"The one that lets you see and feel, and share with us—Southcrop Vision! Will you help us?" Auja gave him a chance to think it over. He said nothing. She prodded him further.

"How about it little Fur? Will you go to Deep Sky?"

Fur did not respond. *I give up. What drives this creature?* Auja wondered. She remembered some of his very first words and had an idea. "What about the sun?" she asked Fur. "I thought you were trying to reach it? If you go, I'll help you find your wings. We all will."

There was the longest pause. Auja was in agony. She had let everyone down. Now she had a last chance. If Fur said no, there was nothing more she could do. She would have failed completely.

Just then a large dragonfly shot through the glade, firing brilliant blue-green sunbeams from its shimmering body. It was gone in a flash but caught Fur's attention. His crawlers all stood up at once for a look. "What was that?!" he asked.

"Mosquito Hawk. A green darner,"[42] replied Auja without much interest.

"Wow! Great wings. Wish I could do that. Where's it going in such a rush?"

"Looks like westward to hunt by the Rapids Trail," she replied. "Maybe you'd like to follow it?" she added more hopefully.

"What's a trail?"

"You'll find out if you go."

"Fine."

"What did you say?"

"O.K. I'll go—but how? What should I do?"

A wave of relief swept over Auja. *More than one way to skin a mammal,* she thought.[43] She had accomplished her task. It took far longer than expected, and in the end maybe too long, but she did it without lies. "All in good time," she replied. "But like I said, you can start by following the green darner."

"When?" asked Fur.

"Now!" replied Auja.

"Am I to leave this place forever?" he asked.

"Yes … and no, not entirely. You can visit anytime you like," she replied.

"How?"

"Use Southcrop Vision."

"You know I can't do that without you."

"Do I now? Well, I'll teach you. You haven't seen anything yet. Our senses will be your senses. You'll be free to wander within the forest web, wherever our lines run true. You'll be one of us—Fur of Southcrop. You'll be able to visit me and roam free. Now there's no time for long goodbyes. Hurry up then, before plague does spread to my branches. Goodbye, little Fur."

"Goodbye," he replied. His little voice was shaky, and so too were his crawlers.

"Make sure you stick to the tree canopy wherever you can." Auja could not help giving this last piece of advice.

"Sure."

"Travel in the understorey only when you absolutely have to," she added, not wanting to be guilty of letting him loose without the right cautions.

"All right."

"And of course, stay away from bare rock and forest floor," she added.

"Will do."

"Oh, and steer clear of other caterpillars and the tops of trees as well. That's where crawlers go to die from plague."

"All right already! I thought you said it was time to leave?"

"Yes, quite right. Good luck," she said, not wanting to let go. She had to admit, she had grown fond of this creature.

Auja watched as Fur's crawlers stopped eating and one by one crawled away in single file, leaving their silk resting pad and chewed leaves behind. They came to a twig that pointed up and followed its course.

It was only once the whole colony had departed that Auja could see the full extent of Fur's losses. Obviously, Fur's ox-like defence had done little to help. Many of his crawlers were left behind in various stages of slow-death. The abandoned site was littered with their mummified corpses—eaten from the inside out by rogue wasps. It would take another half-moon[44] before the adult wasps would emerge, but the killing had already begun.

It was nothing out of the ordinary for tent caterpillars. But it was a reality check for Auja. Her small success only marked the beginning of a dangerous quest. There would be enemies hunting little Fur every step of his journey. He was almost sure to perish along with the other tent caterpillars in the forest. The trees' final hope rested on such a slender chance. And time was quickly running out.

But for the moment, Fur was alive. There was nothing else to do but have him forge ahead. Auja watched as the caterpillars crept along her outstretched bough to a branch and a twig, then a leaf that touched neighbour aspen. She felt the last of Fur's tiny tickling feet as he left his birthplace for good. He crawled from aspen to neighbour oak—and kept going—across green-tipped wooden sky-bridges, beyond Auja's glade and on into the depths of the forest.

Part II:
The Long Crawl

The Winding Way

"No rest for me. Always marching. Marching here, marching there, never getting anywhere. My legs are killing me," said little Fur to any tree that cared to listen. He had thousands of legs[45] and every one was sore. It was four days since his departure, and he now understood what he had agreed to do for his tall green friends—give up leisurely leaf nibbling and lolling about for this never ending slog.

Fur's chosen paths were torturously windy. No straight line crawling for him. No bursts and bounds from tree to tree with reckless ease like the squirrels. The terrain was too bumpy. His tiny strides followed stick and leaf too closely. It was a plain fact—the smaller the creature, the further it must go.[46] And he was small. He could gather up all his crawlers and fit onto a single oak leaf.

Little Fur stopped in a perfect patch of afternoon sun on a young aspen. He stretched out his crawlers and waited until he felt the warmth trickle down from fur to skin. Then he pulled his many bodies in tight so the heat could spread evenly amongst them. His innards began to warm too. That felt good.

Now it was time for some treats. When it came to food, nothing compared to red oak. It was his first love and he owed many thanks to Auja for making him so strong. But lately in his travels he had tasted other fare and had to admit—he was fond of trembling aspen.

Aspen was less succulent, but sweet and delicate and so easy to cut through. And the quivering leaves reminded him of wings. It was like dining in the sky amidst flocks of fluttering butterflies. He found aspen leaves easier to manage with their soft curving edges. Oak had all those pointy lobes that made his crawlers butt heads while feeding.

No head butting today. There was nothing but sun and round food. Times like these, it was so easy for Fur to leave behind the worry, to lose himself in the moment and just be. It was enough to make him stay put for good. He could find the sun from here as easily as elsewhere.

But he drove that thought from his mind. He had tried giving up only yesterday. As soon as he had spoken of his wish to stop, his dinner leaf turned sour. And then once again the trees passed their dreadful feelings of sadness to him. It was easier to bear his own distress than that of an entire forest.

Auja had promised him a special treat if he made it to the man-trail, which if all went well he would reach by day's end. He was not sure what this man-trail was, exactly—something about a path to water for large mammals. The trees had shown him pictures using their Southcrop Vision. He saw a narrow clearing, nothing more. There was something ominous about it, though he did not know why. It looked as if there was plenty of sun and tasty young trees for him there. But he had come to understand that the pictures trees sent him were not really pictures at all. They were *perceptions* and so came along with all sorts of extra feelings and meanings attached.

"Hey, Auja," he called out while having a final few nibbles.

"What?" Her voice was as clear and close as if he had never left her boughs.

"I feel the trees are telling me the man-trail is dangerous. Maybe I should stick to the woods instead?"

"No. You can't fly like the crows," replied Auja. "You'll soon enter a land of water and rock. Think your way is winding now, along leaves and twigs, branches and boughs? Try winding your way around lakes and marshes, ponds and bogs, and treeless outcrops of bare rock.

"The trail will be fine as long as you're careful. You can use it to your advantage. It carves a clear and sunny path. You'll be safer from plague, which can't survive in bright sun. You'll have the company of all the forest edge trees. Aspen and cherry, hawthorn and willow, serviceberry and birch will be there for you. Maybe you'll even get to see rollers."

"What's a roller?" Little Fur didn't like the sound of that at all.

"A machine," Auja replied.

"Never heard of them either," said Fur. "What're they for?"

"Rolling. The hewmen use them to travel along their false-rock trails. Hewmen are the greatest rollers in the world. They roll more than they use their own two feet."

Little Fur was familiar with walking, crawling, jumping, flapping, fluttering and even slithering (he had spotted a garter snake down in the leaf litter only two days ago)—but he had never heard of rolling nor of two-footed hewmen that rolled. Auja knew everything. Fur was simple. But he could put two and two together. *Two-footed creatures? Must be some kind of bird*, he thought. "Why roll? Why don't the hewmen fly?" he asked Auja.

"They're not birds. They're large mammals," Auja replied.

Big, two-footed mammals? That sounded weird and awkward too. Rolling must work better. That must be why they rolled. "I'd like to see some hewmen," Fur said.

"Be careful what you wish for. They're dangerous," Auja said.

"What could a mammal do to a tree?" asked Fur.

Auja's leaves rustled but she did not answer. "Come on little Fur, it's time to go. Remember my promise. If you make it to the man-trail, I'll have something special for you."

"What is it?" asked Fur. Trees were full of surprises.

"Time to widen your horizons," replied Auja.

What was that supposed to mean? The sooner Fur got to this trail, the sooner he would know, and so off he went. He crawled and crawled until the forest shadows grew long and lean. He finally stopped before dusk, to eat the tops of a tall sugar maple. He could see the man-trail from where he sat. Tomorrow he would take a closer look. While chomping on young leaves, he watched the distant trees bite slivers in the sun before they swallowed it up. *Widen my horizons? No way Auja beats this view.*

Wider Horizons

Despite what Guide Oak had said at the Gathering, Auja's job did not end when Fur left her boughs. Fur called for her at least once a day and they spent much of their time chatting through the forest web. *What's so special about me?* Auja wondered. Surely he would have met more interesting trees by now.

It must be imprinting.[47] Fur was born in her branches. Auja was the first tree Fur had ever tasted. He probably felt most comfortable with her.

That was fine with Auja. She wanted to keep this creature alive and on track. She had been watching Fur for days, secretly cheering him on from tree to tree and fretting over every obstacle he encountered. He had reached the man-trail. Good for Fur. Time to take him on a wild ride.

☼

"Hey, Auja," Fur called through the forest web, "I made it by sunset as planned. You've got something for me, eh? Better be good after all that crawling." Fur was exhausted and knew Auja's surprise was all that had kept him going so long and late in the day.

"Yes, I hope it was and soon will be. You've already swallowed it. Good night and rest well!" said Auja.

"Hey, what do you mean?" he asked. There was no reply. He called out for Auja again as he took a few last bites of his late dinner. The trees were silent. Had she tricked him?

Fur slinked off his half-eaten leaf and found a broad branch to curl up on. He tried to forget the broken promise as he watched the last of the evening birds sweep midge and mosquito from a dark sky. Funny thing—these birds had smooth wings and furry bodies. In fact, they looked more like mammals. Walking, running, leaping and bounding, rolling and now flying? Mammals could do it all. Then again, trees went where they pleased without ever moving. *Rather be a tree*, he thought as he drifted to sleep.

☼

Ouch, my stomachs are killing me. Some treat, Fur thought. The maple leaves must have been off. Was this pain fair reward for his long day's crawl? The morning light was already strong. *Wow, must've really slept in.* But something was not quite right. It felt like tomorrow had come before yesterday was through. Fur looked at the sunrise. *Hang on, that's not east.*

The sun was in the wrong place, and it was going the wrong way—down! Fur scanned the trees around him, trying to regain his bearings. He saw a tall sugar maple. That tree looked familiar. There was a crawler colony at the top of maple's crown. That colony looked familiar too. It was Fur! He understood. It was Southcrop Vision. He had swallowed these pictures at dinner. There had been a delay like the last time, but now, in the middle of the night, he could finally see them.

The trees carried Fur away. This time they took him much faster and further. He was a goshawk bolting through the forest. It felt so real it made his innards churn. Some of his crawlers even threw up. Black sticky bile bubbled from his mouths. But he knew he was not really moving. He was curled up and cozy in sugar maple. With this thought in mind, he began to enjoy the thrill of the ride.

Forget goshawk, he flew faster than any bird toward the sunset. Everything beneath slipped by in a blur. He saw hardwoods and water and rock. Then a clearing appeared, like the man-trail he had seen from maple's crown. But this one was smooth and very wide and covered in black filth that reeked. *Must be false-rock.*

The foul smell got worse as a herd of shining creatures appeared. They sat on round black rocks that spun round while they moved at great speed. He figured they must be rollers. *What noisy, stinking beasts.* There was little time to look and no hewmen to see as the machines disappeared in a flash. Their stench lingered.

Fur saw big water beyond the roller trail. It looked like it went on forever. Maybe it was Lake Attigouatan? He wanted a better look but could not cross the false-rock. He turned from the trail and soared through a red oak forest that ended at the banks of a wide river. He followed it eastward, along hard rock edges and hidden wetlands that lay tucked away beyond the main channel.

The river banks and even the river itself were littered with bright-coloured shapes. They were smooth and simple and had sharp edges. Some looked like rollers but did not roll. No time to inspect. The trees pushed and pulled him.

Fur came to another clearing. This one was thin and had sparkling lines of silver running through. The lines stretched over the river along a bridge of smooth grey criss-crossed logs, then disappeared into the bush on the other side. He thought he might like to follow them across but had no control over which way he went. Others were leading. He must follow.

He left the river and followed the silver lines south and eastward, gliding by their sides through stands of aspen and cherry. He saw more and more hewmen trails. They slowed him down. He leapt over and under them; he was not sure how. Then he remembered what Auja had once told him. *'Through leaves and roots and the soil surrounds.'* If this was the way trees spoke to each other, then Southcrop Vision must work the same way.

Fur was stopped by a big man-trail like the other he had visited to the west. It was jam packed with lines of rollers, and the air was thick with filth. The scenery was so dreary. Row after row of drab structures covered the land. False-rock smothered everything.

Across the trail there was more big water. He followed the trail for a long while, racing rollers from its side. The near and far shores of the water nearly touched before giving way to an endless sea.

Fur arrived at the edge of a forest and could go no further. Open fields and sad, lonely trees lay before him. The wild lands were gone. His voyage was over.

What a ride. What a thrill, he thought as his mind returned to his bodies in the sugar maple. He gasped with excitement as his crawlers pushed and shoved and squirmed about. There was more to life than crawling! With his tree friends, he could grab up the big, wide world and explore it without ever moving.

But trees did not stand everywhere. And the ones that remained in Southcrop were far from happy. He could feel their pain. It came wrapped up with all the other sensations they had shared with him. Most had abandoned all hope. They only wished for the quick end so they might finally lie down and leave their gloomy earth behind.

☼

"Wake up! Wake up!" someone shouted at Fur.

Fur was groggy and the harsh glare of morning sun did not help. Last night's 'dream' hung over him like a fog. He wanted to crawl into shade and go back to sleep.

"Come on, you lazy lump of crawlers! You've slept long enough!"

Who was yelling at him, and, more importantly, how could he hear whomever it was? He was not eating (he was barely awake).

"Is that you, Auja?"

"Yes. Now get up. You're wasting travel time."

Last night was enough of a surprise. Auja had come through with her promise and then some. But now there was more—surprise, part two.

"How's it possible?" Fur asked.

"What?"

"I can hear you talking, but I'm not chewing leaves."

"No longer necessary, as long as you stick to us trees."

"How does that work?" asked Fur.

"Mostly through the pores[48] on our leaves and stems. Guide Oak showed me how. She said the time was right, and she's given you full access."

"Why?"

"We believe in you," replied Auja. "You've made it this far without wandering off. You're one of us now."

Fur was thrilled with his new powers. He could speak freely whenever he wished. Could he do the same with Southcrop Vision? What if he could travel where he pleased? What if? His spirits soared.

"Thank you, thank you, and for last night too," said Fur.

"You're very welcome. So what do you think of Southcrop Vision now?" asked Auja.

"Amazing!" said Fur "You can really *see* and fly too, faster than birds."

"Like I said, we don't actually fly."

"Whatever, you share. Oh, the things I saw!" Fur felt an emptiness gnawing at his guts as he spoke. Last night's 'flying' was hungry work. He pulled himself into a line and quickly marched towards breakfast. The words spilled out as he crawled. "Oh and Auja, I saw rollers and … long silver lines, and all kinds of unnatural shapes—on water and riverbanks. Are they from the hewmen world too?"

"Yes," replied Auja, "floats for water travel and shelters to live in. And wait and see the roller that rolls along the shiny silver!"

Rollers for rolling. Floats for … floating? He would have to add 'floating' to his 'ways to move' list.

"Was that a hewmen colony I saw by the eastern big water?" he asked Auja.

"I guess you could call it that. That was Mnjikaning,[49] a hewmen gathering place at the narrows between Windy Bay and Ouentironk."

"What about those fields I saw to the south?" asked Fur. "There were no flowers, herbs, grasses or shrubs. They didn't look natural."

"Hewmen farms," said Auja. "There they grow crops and raise birds and mammals for food."

Farms? The 'others' spoke this word often. (The 'others' were the whispering tree voices that had followed little Fur since he began his quest. They mostly sounded like leaf rustle and wind, but sometimes he would catch a word or phrase.) Farms were on the minds of many in Southcrop.

"Is that where I'm headed?" Fur asked Auja. She was silent. "Hey Auja, am I going to the farms?"

"A farm?" Auja replied "Hmm … yes, that's where you're going, but it's nothing like the ones you saw."

"Show me!"

"You'll have to see for yourself. And if we waste any more time chatting, you never will. The sun is high. Best be on your way."

The Rapids Trail

Fur had grown accustomed to the man-trail. Auja had been right. It eased the way. It cut a clear and sunny path. Tasty friends lined the way.

He spoke with each tree he passed. They were always polite and kept him in good company. And even in his quietest moments, the 'others' were with him. Their voices and song would brush him like breezes whether he was toiling and crawling in the scorch of sun or drifting to sleep under the sparkling expanse.

But Auja remained Fur's closest companion. She was always willing to come when called and entertain his questions, no matter how outlandish. They flitted and fluttered across the surface of things. Fur's life was too short. He wanted essence without detail—to see and know all without lingering. He felt Auja wanted the same.

Of course, Auja could drone on for ever if left unchecked. She was long-lived so was bound to be long-winded. But beneath her tree-ness she was a flighty thing. Fur had heard enough dull conversations to understand this. And he thanked his mother for laying him in Auja and not some tedious tree. Fur and Auja were kindred spirits living their lives along different scales of time.

"You don't say?! Amazing! Fantastic! Could it really be as simple as that?" Fur said one warm, pleasant evening as Auja explained the rules of fern growth and form. "Now what about that? I see the same thing over there. Are the rules the same there as here?"

"Where?"

"There, up high."

"I thought we were looking down here. I thought you were asking about the forest floor ferns," said Auja.

"Yes, yes, I was. But we're done, aren't we? If I let you keep going, I'll be long dead before you're done. So now I'm looking up there. Come on. Use those bright green leaves of yours. Way up. See those feathery clouds? Tell me, how are they made? How do they grow and form?"

☼

It was time for Fur to moult once again. He stretched. His crawlers wreathed and pushed and puffed themselves up. Their tight skins cracked and split. Out popped big heads and new furry skins. He had reached his fourth crawler stage. *Ah, feels good. New fur and more room to grow.*

Fur checked himself over. He had sick crawlers—infected by wasps and flies and other nasty parasites—but there was no sign of plague. And he numbered over two hundred healthy and strong.

His thoughts turned to his next meal. Times like these, he wished he could see like trees whenever he wanted so he could find the best patches without having to search. He saw a horde of shimmering leaves in the aspen bough above. They looked tasty. He had better check them out to be sure.

He gathered his crawlers for the march to the aspen's main trunk, up to the bough and out to the green target he had in his sights. Problem was, his target was moving. So too were aspen's branches, then the whole tree as well. Even his view of the forest was shifting. Suddenly, the leaves he was chasing were right in front of him. And he could smell them too. They were perfect for eating.

How'd I get here? he wondered. *Southcrop Vision, that's how.* He forgot about food. He was too excited to eat and he had to be sure. *Go up to the top.* He floated to the tip of aspen's highest branch. Amazing! His wish had come true. He could now use Southcrop Vision to go where he pleased. Even better, there was no delay. The Southcrop sensations came straight away!

I want to see myself. Fur dropped through aspen's crown and stopped by a sunny patch of west facing trunk. He, the colony was settled in nicely where tree trunk met limb.

He was presently shaped like a crescent moon and appeared large and imposing. From a distance, he might be mistaken for a squirrel but was far more impressive. His dark bodies were studded with vivid blue and white markings arranged in neat lines that gleamed from his fresh rough of fur. Fur remembered how tiny he had been when he first emerged in early spring. Despite exhausting days of endless crawling, he had managed to find energy to grow. What a striking beast he was.

Take me to oak tree, Fur thought, catching sight of aspen's neighbour and wanting to push this further. No go. His mind returned to the colony. *Can't jump yet, but I can see like the trees.*

☼

The sun had almost set on the eighteenth day of Fur's long crawl. Fur had stopped in a cherry tree for the night. It was slender and small and could offer two meals at best. But cherry's leaves would no doubt be tasty.

Fur's fourth stage coats were filling in nicely—maybe too nicely. He was running out of time. He had done well to get this far, but the hardest parts of his journey lay ahead. He was restless and this feeling would only get worse as he grew. Soon his crawlers would want to leave. In the end, he would have to let them—tent caterpillars spend their final crawler days alone. But first he had to get across Oak River.

The trees were helping him every step of the way, as Auja had promised. He remembered all the dead crawlers he had seen on his journey—broken bodies strewn about the forest, whole families wiped out in their prime. And that was only the start. The trees sent him images of the gathering storm. Flies and wasps and even small mammals were on the hunt and closing in. He needed the trees' help to survive. He had to stick with their plan.

Delicious, he thought as he relished the sweet juice of the last few cherry leaves within reach. He lay there splayed out, with furry crawlers engulfing an entire branch of the young cherry. Her leaves were special. She had prepared them for him. Trees could direct which ways their branches grew. They could sprout leaves wherever they saw fit and control the flow of nutrients to each.

But cherries had an extra-special talent. They knew exactly what tent caterpillars liked. There was never any need for food searching while in the boughs of such trees. They could lay out sunny-side paths lined with the finest leafy treats.

As the last of the nearby leaf morsels were now gone, Fur considered his next move. A lone white birch stood along the Rapids Trail ahead. He was supposed to reach her by tomorrow afternoon, spend the night and then leave the trail and turn back into the forest. He could clearly see the birch from his vantage; her white trunk shone in the fading light. But between them lay a wetland, complete with rushes, standing dead trees and some straggly black spruce and tamarack who, by the looks of things, were barely hanging on for dear life.

Fur was told to stay put for the night and then crawl around the wetland tomorrow along its tree-lined edges. He usually listened without question. But there was a simpler and faster route. He could take the man-trail over the water. If he left now, he might reach white birch in time for a late snack. But it was already getting dark. He was never to travel at night. He was never to leave the reach of the forest web.

Fur spotted a pair of rollers off in the distance. Each carried two pieces of sun. It was not his first sighting, but rollers were rare on this small and bumpy trail. Despite the noise and smell, they always gave him a thrill.

Fur had been warned to stay away from the trailside. Rollers were dangerous and could attack without warning. The lure of their false-light could lead to tragedy. He did not care. He wanted to take the shortcut. And if he hurried he might get a closer look at those oncoming sunbeams. False or not, he could not resist. He made up his mind. He would go for it.

Once down from the trees, it was the grasses that gave Fur the most trouble as he felt his way in the dark. The trees shouted at him to stop. Their voices were faint, and then they disappeared altogether as he left the forest web behind. He wished the trees could understand. He had to see the night-time sun.

Fur reached the trail's edge where it was easy to walk. *Hah! No problem*, he thought. By this time the first roller had arrived. The glare of light halted him there as it zoomed by. The beams of the next one were now approaching. He had to get closer. He reached out for the middle of the trail with a long line of crawlers. He looked back and saw two giant circles of white light. The dark retreated. He could see the trailside wall of willow shrubs exposed in the eerie glow. Then the lights rushed upon him. He was blinded by their brilliance. They were beautiful!

There was a thunderous rumble that grew louder and louder. Then a sudden and terrible, burning pain ripped through him as he was crushed by the speeding roller. This was nothing like the slow sickness of infection from rogue wasps—nothing like the numbing sting of soldier bug attacks. This death was sudden and sharp.

The roller was gone, but a fresh glow creeping along the trail from behind told of another on its way. He caught a glimpse of his flattened crawler corpses crushed into the trail—their blood and guts glistening in the oncoming light. He lost his bearings as his fear and the agony of his wounds overcame him. Again, the white circles of light grew larger as the roller drew nearer.

Must get away. He turned himself around and raced toward the trail's edge. The roller bore down upon him. He could feel the blast of air sweep his fur. Then it was gone.

Fur did not stop. He limped along as fast as he could away from the man-trail, through the tough grasses, and up a tree. He was battered by a sudden rush of tree voices but ignored them. Only after the last of his feet were safely on tree bark did he halt. Then he collapsed in a quivering heap of fur.

☼

Auja had watched the terrible events of last night unfold. She had been called in to make Fur stop, but too late, and arrived only in time to see him grappling with the trailside grasses.

She screamed but knew he was beyond hearing. Then she watched helplessly as the line of crawlers veered into the path of the oncoming roller. Using the leaves of the roadside trees at the scene, Auja found the best vantage and trained all her senses on that horrible moment. Time seemed to slow and linger as if to prolong her agony. She could almost hear the sound of soft bodies burst as the crushing weight of the roller bore down upon Fur. Then time returned to its usual course, the roller passed and she saw the remains—flattened bodies, the blood-stained trail and Fur's confused retreat.

Fool, she thought. Fur had ignored their warnings and ran off to chase rollers. To make matters worse, after almost making it to white birch he had run for dear life *back* to the cherry he had started from. It had all been for naught.

The rest of Southcrop was angry as well, but not with Fur. "Foolish tree! Need I remind you your task is not over?" Guide Oak said to Auja. Then her tone softened. "You must watch over the Rune creature. You have a special bond. We cannot do this without you." The rest of the elders spoke their minds too, but with less kindness.

Once Fur had returned, all of Southcrop Forest called out to him. They cried and pleaded all night and into the morning.

☼

Where am I? Who's shouting? Where's my oak? Fur recognized one voice. Unlike the others it was soothing and friendly. It was Auja. Auja was a tree—his oak tree. She was his friend. He was meant to help her.

Fur knew this little cherry as well. He had eaten her before—recently, by the looks of the chewed leaves and silk trails. Then he remembered the events of the night before. Maybe it had been a bad dream? He felt for his healthy crawlers. There were two hundred and twelve—same as yesterday. He tried to move each one to be sure.

All was not well. A part of him had gone numb. He checked himself again, this time by looking each crawler over as he counted. There were only one hundred and seventy-two. He was forty short. His mind was playing tricks. He tried once more—forty short again. It had not been a dream. Those forty crawlers were dead. His mind was simply slow to catch on. They had become his phantom limbs—there in spirit but not in body.

Fur was horrified. He had made a terrible mistake. He had been trampled by a roller and was lucky to be alive. He was back in cherry with nothing to eat. He had let the trees down and had lost precious time. It was time to go.

Fur drew his crawlers in tight before starting his march. He tugged at his phantoms as well. They shot back with vicious barbs of pain. He tried to move without pulling at his wounds but could not distinguish between his living and dead parts. The searing pain cut his feet from beneath him. He was not going anywhere. *Forty phantoms to haunt me.* He lost consciousness.

Foul Weather

Fur awoke to sharp red beams from above as sun and cloud battled for the skies.

"Morning, little Fur. How are you feeling?" asked Auja.

"O.K., I think," he replied.

"Good! You've got to move on. The weather is turning, and you've nothing left to eat here."

"What, already? It's early," he said.

"Early? You've been asleep since yesterday morning!"

"What the ...?" Fur scanned his surroundings, confused at first. Then once again he remembered. Auja was right. Better get crawling. Fur had discovered the hard way what could happen if he ignored her wise words.

He flexed his crawlers. His wounds ached and throbbed as he struggled to move, but the pain had lost some of its bite. He found he was able to walk—slowly at first, as he fought to keep his crawlers in line. The loss of so many had weakened his control. And he tripped and stumbled over his new phantom limbs.

This time Fur took the long, safe route through the upper canopy of trees that skirted the wetland. As he travelled he saw hoards of caterpillars amassed on the tree trunks below. In his pain and fatigue, he felt a strong urge to let go and join them, but the trees would not hear of it. The dangers of plague were ever present. And there was no time to tarry, as he had lost precious time. He had already moved far enough for three generations of his kind. Not good enough. Despite injury he had to keep up the furious pace.

By late afternoon Fur had almost made it back to the Rapids Trail. The sky had grown very dark, and the clouds looked so heavy they seemed bound to fall and strike the earth. The trees pleaded with him to hurry. He was in danger. Violent weather was on the way.

"Don't you think it would be safer to stay here?" he asked Auja. "Those trees by the trail are so exposed."

"We've talked it over. You've already lost too much time. You should be fine in white birch," Auja replied.

Fur took a good look at his soon-to-be host, who stood at the edge of a hemlock and balsam fir grove. Birch was a sturdy but graceful queen, a strong but delicate beauty. She had small heart-shaped leaves on drooping twigs and branches and creamy white bark that peeled in thin sheets. Her striking pose was hard to miss, with her bright bark shining out against the dark green behind her.

Graceful yes, but she did not look like good shelter. She grew too close to the open trail and was surrounded by harsh, foodless needle-bearers. But there was no time to question the trees' choice. The storm was nearly upon him. He could feel it in the air.

Fur reached the white birch and crawled on to her blazing bark, in the nick of time. He gave the birch a curt 'hello' as he rushed up her trunk. He then gathered his crawlers in close and braced himself for the worst.

The sky unleashed its energy with great fury. It was the strongest wind he had ever felt. It pried at his feet, trying to rip them from bark and fling his crawler bodies into the churning chaos. The driving rain soaked right through to his skins, chilling him to the core. He shivered and twitched with cold and fear.

The full force of the storm slammed into the birch and tore one of her branches clear from her trunk. She groaned in pain. Fur watched with dread. Three of his crawlers still clung to the branch as the wind hurled it into a water-filled ditch. *Three more phantoms to join with the others. Three more to haunt me.*

☼

The worst of the storm had passed but the cold and wet lingered, making travel impossible. It was too early for the hot smother of damp weather in summer. Fur stayed on with the birch, mostly holed up as the bitter winds and sheets of driving rain battered him. He could do little in this foul weather except:

1. eat (of course) whenever possible,

2. sleep,

3. sulk,

4. and, for more positive activity, practice tree 'jumping' through root and leaf. (He was a very quick learner and could now 'leap' from tree to tree.)

Fur was thrilled with his growing power to use Southcrop Vision. Eating and sleeping were fine too. But he would rather have avoided the sulking. He wished he could believe that all was O.K. His loss from the storm was nothing compared to that roller trampling. A few crawlers here, a few crawlers there—what did it really matter?

These were hollow thoughts. If he kept losing a few here and there he would end up a phantom himself. Fur was more than the sum of his parts, but without enough parts he would cease to be.

What troubled Fur most was the way he had lost those three caterpillars. The trees had failed him. He had followed Auja's lead. She had told him to take cover in that birch, and he could have been killed. Two days of wet chill was starting to get to him. He had trouble moving and even digesting. He was miserable, so he went after his closest friend.

"Hey, Auja. Why didn't you see that storm coming?"

"We did," she replied in an instant.

She's always watching and listening, Fur thought. "Not fast enough for me," he replied.

"You're right, I'm sorry."

"Why did you tell me to run for the white birch? The storm hit her straight on. I thought you trees knew everything?"

"Who told you that? We made a mistake. The storm veered towards you at the last moment. It was impossible to predict," Auja said.

"Didn't you once tell me the sun drives our weather—that it moves air and water?" asked Fur.

"Yes."

Didn't you say it keeps our world in order?"

"It's true!"

"What order? You can't even tell where the storms will strike!"

"You know, little Fur," said Auja, "not everything's as simple as days and seasons. There's plenty of surprise too. Remember my mother's words? 'Nothing in life's for certain. That's what makes life worth living.' Imagine the world without the unexpected. If we could see the end, right from the start, life would be ever so dull. Is that what you'd like?"

"Well ... not really. But I don't like surprises that end with dead crawlers," Fur replied.

"Ha, you can't pick and choose. You'll have to take the good with the bad," said Auja.

So Fur's leafy companions were not perfect. They made mistakes. Sure, they were smart and powerful and would do their best to keep him alive, but they did not know everything. Fur's life was his own to look after. Best to keep his wits about him else he would never reach the sun.

Fur noticed the rain was letting up. The sky was much brighter and a blast of dry air brushed his fur. "Look's like the weather's clearing. Now there's a happy surprise," he said. The sun dipped below the treetops while its rays bounced off the cloud bottoms. He had better get some rest. He would soon be on the move again.

Hewmen

Rollers! Fur saw the telltale glow creeping over the crest of a hill as he was drifting off to sleep in the white birch. Then the blinding white circles of light appeared.

After all Fur had been through, he still felt the lure of the false-lights. Soon there would be the rumble noise. Then he would feel a blast of air across his fur, the roller would speed by and the red glow of its rear would signal its passing.

Something's not right. The white circles did not speed. In fact, they began to slow. Fur watched as the roller glided to a halt beneath him. The rumbling stopped. It took him some time to adjust to the lights, but what he saw next took his breath away and made his crawlers shiver and their hairs quiver with fear. A piece of the stalled roller peeled off its side—like a shiny strip of bark from a white birch trunk. Two large creatures emerged, stood face to face and began to squawk loudly.

☼

"Come on, you told me this road was O. K.!"

"It was, until that storm hit."

"Yeah right, maybe in first gear at a mile an hour. There are pot-holes everywhere. Need a hummer for this. We're gonna' have to turn back before it gets too dark."

"What? We've been at it for hours. No way!"

"No way? Are you paying for all the damage to the rental, eh?"

"What damage? Looks good as new and we're almost there."

"Almost where?! You've got no idea. The next pothole will swallow our car!"

The two argued a while longer. Then they got back in the car, turned it around and drove back the way they had come.

☼

Ach, hewmen, Auja thought as she borrowed birch's leaves to have a closer look. Their hairless flesh and meaty stench always made her uneasy. And why not? They were unpredictable creatures and could fell a tree with ease. The birch had called for Auja as soon as the roller had stopped. That was good thinking. Who knew what Fur might do? Maybe he would be foolish enough to crawl out and greet them.

"Hello, little Fur," said Auja. What's all the excitement?"

"Hewmen. I saw some!" Fur said.

Auja had given Fur tours of the animal kingdom, sending him images whenever he asked. But she had always left hewmen out of the show. She no longer considered them part of the forest.

Auja could sense Fur's excitement. The little leaves of white birch bounced up and down as Fur's crawlers ran back and forth from twig to twig. Through white birch and the wonders of Southcrop Vision, Auja could feel his crawler feet as they scraped and tugged at birch's bright bark and green.

"Right you are. They're people—the hewmen people," said Auja.

"They looked colourful and clumsy and ... and ..."

"Unnatural?" Auja said, helping Fur to finish. "Those colours were not theirs. They belong to the false skin and fur they wear to keep warm and dry. They're weak and ill-suited for life in these parts."

"Their heads look too big for their bodies!" added Fur.

"Big heads for big brains. Did you notice their hands?"

"I think so—like the squirrels have."

"Oh no, they're very different," said Auja. "They can do much more than grab and clutch and cling. Their hands are the tools used to wield the power of their minds."

"Where do the hewmen come from?" asked Fur.

"Almost everywhere these days. But most travel up from the south, down by Toronton."[50]

"Toronton? I thought you said their colony was called Mnjikaning?" Fur asked.

"They have many colonies. Toronton is much larger and further away. It's a vast meeting place teaming with millions by the shores of Onitariio," Auja replied. [51] "There live peoples from all ends of this earth, amongst the lingering remains of a once grand hardwood forest. It used to be a most beautiful place."

Auja knew she was heading for trouble. Every time she thought about hewmen the rage would well up inside. She could feel her sap warm as she spoke. "I wonder if the rivers and ravines of Toronton run true to this day. Do the mighty oak stand atop the hill's crest over the old lake shore?[52] Not likely. The trees of Toronton are old and sick. The air's no longer fit to breathe. They're all dying." Auja's leaves bristled with anger as she spoke.

"Look to the south. Can you see it? Do you feel it? Hewmen poisons paint the sky. They'll destroy us all." Auja shook her south-facing branches toward the dirty, pink pall that smothered the twilight. "Their machines began spewing their filth a century ago, fouling the air as they burned. It hasn't stopped since. It only gets worse."

"Are the hewmen your enemies?" said Fur.

"Some are, other aren't and most simply don't care about us. It wasn't always this way," she replied.

"Why? What happened?" asked Fur.

Auja knew that answering would bring back more feelings best left buried inside. Too late—they had already burst out. She began her sad tale. "It is said in their beginnings they came from our branches. But that was a very long time ago. They first became common in these parts after the Big Ice."

"What were they like?" asked Fur.

"The first people were social—they needed each other, like they do now."

"Like the tent caterpillars, eh?"

"Well yes, sort of, in a way," she replied and then chuckled to herself at Fur's odd suggestion.

"Through the wonders of their cooperation, they rose above their meek bodies and became a powerful force. They had their ugly sides too—always fighting and killing. What do you expect from the mammals after all? But a bond grew between us nonetheless. It was because they were a part of the forests. They knew the ways of all the animals and plants. With trees and peoples living side by side, it was only a matter of time. We came to understand each other. And there was contact!"

"What? You talk to hewmen?" Fur asked.

"No, not anymore. But we used to, before going our separate ways."

"What happened then?" asked Fur.

"Hmm. Let's see. It began about four centuries ago. That's when we first spotted trouble. It was the beginning of the great hewmen age—their age of greed," Auja replied.

"What's greed?"

"They take more than they need. They hoard and consume and always want more," she said.

"What went wrong?" Fur asked.

Auja could tell that little Fur was thoroughly engaged. His crawlers had by now retreated to birch's upper trunk and had drawn together in a tight circle. He was perfectly still.

"At the time we were closest with the Wendat[53] people, who were common in these parts, and we were friendly with the Anishinabek,[54] who roamed the granite shield to the north. Suddenly, strange foods and killing tools appeared along their trade routes. We'd never seen anything like them before. We should've known that trouble was coming."

"What trouble?"

It was a most uncomfortable subject. But Auja had to admit, she was enjoying her captive audience. It was so rare to find anyone who would listen to her and for what?—a basic lesson in history that every youngster knew all too well.

"The explorers!" she said finally. "They came to Southcrop from beyond the eastern salt sea by way of Lake Attigouatan and the northern river route.[55] And somewhere along the way they found something they couldn't resist. The desire for it consumed them and changed our world forever."

"What was it? Tell me!" little Fur pleaded.

Auja paused for a moment as something pleasing had caught her eye much closer to home. It made her feel better after all the hewmen talk. "A queen bumble bee," she blurted out. She had become distracted by a very large bee that lumbered through her glade on its way home for the night.

Such a busy queen. She was lucky enough to survive the winter freeze, and for what—to struggle and toil to found her new colony. She could pass much of the hard work off to her daughters once hatched, but for now had to go at it alone. Auja was fond of these insects and was never too busy to watch one at work.

"Bumble bee? What are you talking about, eh?" Fur asked. His crawlers twitched and wriggled about.

"So sorry, got distracted," said Auja. "Beaver," she added.

"Beaver? Bees, beavers—what next? Is your mind wandering?" Fur asked.

"No it's not. That's what I meant to say—beaver."

"What's so special about that big-toothed, flat-tailed, furry, wet mammal?"

"It was all for the sake of their fur," Auja replied. "The explorers took millions of beaver furs in floats—like the ones you saw on Oak River—through the White Bear waters[56] and our River Divide and back across the Eastern Sea."

"Why? What did they need them for?"

"Need? Who said need? Think greed! They wore the beaver fur on their heads. We used to call them the fur-bearing mammals." Auja found this funny and laughed until her leaves shook.

"Why didn't they go for us tent caterpillars? Our colours are much better," said Fur.

That sent a fresh wave of leaf shaking through Auja's crown. But her serious tone quickly returned. "The early explorers were spirited and brave. Didn't they know what their voyages would unleash? The fur trade! These men flooded the first peoples' trade routes with beaver furs. The first peoples helped to trap and move them.

"The beavers could not survive the onslaught. But it wasn't only the beaver that suffered. So too did the first people. They were ravaged by a deadly plague[57] brought by the explorers from overseas. And they were ravaged by wars to control the trade routes. The Haudenosaunee[58] peoples drove the Wendat away. Then next came the Anishinabek from the north. And in the end it didn't matter who won the battles, the fur trade collapsed. Both beaver and first peoples were too few.

"We hoped then that the explorers and traders would leave our lands—but no—they were not finished here. They became settlers and farmers and hewmen. They unleashed themselves upon the fish and the forests—it was about three centuries ago. They feared our wilds because we hindered their farming. We became their resource, as their numbers grew and grew. It was then we said good-bye to the first people—maybe forever more."

"Why? Where'd they go?" Fur asked.

"Don't know. Don't care," Auja replied. "Maybe they're there amongst all the others. They're all the same to us now—all one kind, all wanting more. They're the hewmen. Hewmen, hewmen everywhere and hardly a tree left standing.

"First they hacked down the white pines for their sea floats, and the rest of our kind soon followed to fuel their expansion. It took no more than a century to clear the forests south of the granite, and then the shield trees soon followed. Though many have grown back, we don't grow big or live long like we used to."

Auja was heating up again. Her leaves trembled as her voice quaked. She wanted to stop, but the words spilled out. "And now as the hewmen sprawl creeps up from Toronto, and their machines grow stronger and multiply, we will suffer our greatest loss. They will destroy our farms. And that will be the end of us all."

"What farms? You mean like the one I'm heading for?"

"Yes."

"Why's it so important? Does it hold the secret of Southcrop Vision?"

"Yes, it does," Auja replied.

"Do you grow visions there?"

"You'll find out soon enough."

"What if it's gone, even before I get there?"

Auja's leaves drooped at Fur's question. She could not bear to answer. "Enough hewmen stories," she said. "Off to sleep, my friend. Tomorrow you must crawl."

There was no sense treading further down that sorry path—prodding old wounds, ill-healed after centuries. And yet, like a leaky beaver dam giving way to a surge, Auja's mind could not withstand the current of emotion that swept through her. As she fell asleep she started to dream. Her dream was first fuelled by her own memories of hewmen. Then she borrowed the memories of others.

☼

Fur could not fall asleep after all the excitement. He listened to the white birch instead. Though she had said very little to him since he had arrived, she could make music like no other tree. She mixed in the sounds of the forest—leaf rustle, twig snap, bough break, tree fall—rain splash, stream burble, rapids rush, avalanche. And she added the sounds of life gathered throughout the seasons—snake hiss, owl hoot, cicada hum, grouse drum—warbler warble, pheasant flush, bee buzz—bat peep, nighthawk pee-ik—wolf howl, cat yowl, bear growl—crow caw, frog croak, dove coo—beetle click, cricket chirp, and (he imagined for his own delight) crawler chomp.

Auja's got to hear this. Fur called for her. She did not reply. She was probably asleep. He found something else entirely.

☼

Fur was swept away into a vision-filled night, overcome by the sensations of others. He saw people, but they looked so different from the fat ones that had rolled on the Rapids Trail. These had long black hair and animal skin covers. They were chasing a deer through the bush. They killed it with tall, pointed sticks and smaller ones too that they hurled from bowed branches.

'*Wendat hunters,*' said a voice in his head.

How could that be? Fur knew they had been gone for centuries.

Maybe they're memories, he thought. The images were faded and misty. They felt old and sad. Who in Southcrop could remember such things? It must be Ancient Sugar Maple. She was over four hundred years old.

The scene changed suddenly—to a different place and maybe a different time. Fur spotted a river float with white patches and curved ends. It was covered in birch bark. He found its smooth shape pleasing somehow. There was a person sitting inside. It was covered in false fur except for the face. There were two long twisted strands of hair growing from the head. There were other people on the river bank standing next to a massive pile of beaver furs.

'*Anishinabek,*' said the voice in his head.

Then the scenes switched again and again. He saw men swinging sharp shiny sticks, fallen trees and rivers choked with logs. He saw barren lands with not a tree left standing and soil laid bare to waste.

Why?

'*Think greed,*' said the whispering voice.

The vision ended there. Fur's mind returned to his colony—or that is what he first thought. But when he tried to flex his crawlers, he felt hardwood and roots and stiff green-tipped limbs instead. He was a strapping young oak. He was she. She was Auja. It was Southcrop Vision once again. Fur had tapped into Auja's dream!

Mosquito Hawk

Next morning was warm and calm. Fur awoke before dawn and made each one of his crawlers stand up and sway just to be sure he was himself once again. He was. Last night's adventure was over. It was time to use his own feet. There would be plenty of hard marching ahead.

Not so fast. Fur had some time before sunup for a bit of tree jumping. Maybe he could go a little further this time. How he longed to 'fly' far using Southcrop Vision as the trees had showed him.

He began with a short leap from white birch to hemlock. He could see himself from hemlock's needles. Fur was accustomed to the evergreen view, though it had taken some getting used to. He was a creature of broad leaves.

The evergreens saw things differently. Though they had the advantage of sight all year round, their colour vision was never quite as rich, and the edges of things sometimes looked coarse and fuzzy. But their sense of smell was much stronger. They could catch the scent of flowers and mammals and even birds on the wing from a great distance if the winds were right.

Fur jumped from hemlock to balsam fir to aspen. Then he jumped some more. He went in fits and starts at first but soon caught his rhythm and glided seamlessly from tree to tree.

He was thrilled. He had never gone so far without help. He figured he could go a lot further. Maybe he would visit Auja and the old glade? Maybe he would check the creek for damselflies. His jumps grew faster and longer. The trees whipped by in a blur. He was back in his birthplace in a flash.

"Hello, Fur. Who carried you here?" asked Auja.

There was no hiding from Auja. She must have felt him through the forest web the moment he had arrived. "No one. I came by myself," he replied.

"Well now, you've learned a thing or two," said Auja. "Best be careful. It's your first time so far away from your bodies."

"I'll be quick. I only want to take a peek at the damselflies," Fur said.

"I could show you, you know. All you need do is …" Auja began to say.

Fur left before Auja could finish. A thrill shot through him as he sighted a flock of his favourite insects by the creek. These were no ordinary damselflies. They were the black wings, the most beautiful creatures he had ever seen.[59] They fluttered about the creek on ebony jewels, their bodies glowing iridescent green in the sunlight.

Suddenly, a powerful flying insect zoomed by overhead. "Mosquito hawk, ruler of the skies!" said Fur. It was green darner, the dragonfly. He had met the winged giant only once before—at the very start of his long crawl. He hoped he would see it again someday, and here it was. The darner's flight was nothing like the tepid fluttering of the moths. Its movements were powerful and dexterous. Even the birds were no match. Fur watched as it thrust and darted and dashed upon its supple wings. What an exhibition.

Not bad for an insect, Fur thought. He gave chase. "You're a great flyer, but I'm faster than you," he cried, "I'm not bound by my body. I go where I please. I have no limits. I am the trees!"

Auja called after him "That's far enough. You're going to get lost."

"Yeah, whatever," Fur muttered, and then he was gone. He followed green darner as it sped north through the forest until it reached a pair of silver lines. The dragonfly flew above the lines while Fur pursued from the forest edge. The chase stretched on and on and on. Fur knew he was wasting far too much time but could not resist the dragonfly's lure.

Fur spotted Oak River straight ahead. He could see the bridge where the silver lines crossed. The darner took a quick turn into the forest. Fur followed alongside it, then behind it and in front all at once. It was in full flight but he made it stand still with his ever-shifting tree vantage.

Fur followed the green darner over a high bluff of rock, lichens and sparse oak, down past a dense hemlock grove and along the edge of a clearing lined with cedar and wildflowers beneath. He was struck by the variety of his surroundings. There were so many kinds of places to live and so many different plants and creatures to fill them. The darner zoomed down to a dank wetland and then stopped to hover at the water's edge. Behind it, dead trees stood stark naked in a large beaver pond.

Fur drifted in closer for a look. The damp and dark overcame the bright buzz of spring. Then he saw something that made his skins tingle with fear. For the first time on this jaunt he faltered.

They were rollers, but no ordinary rollers. These ones were monstrous and had long necks and massive jaws lined with sharp, shiny teeth. There were five of them, huddled together, motionless at the far end of the pond. What prey might call this hideous pack to the hunt?

The darner abandoned him there. It streaked through a thicket of alders, over the wetland, and then crossed the river to Deep Sky.

Where am I? Should've listened to Auja. Fur had strayed and was lost and alone. All around him were dying trees and their dead log remains. They were coated with grotesque splotches and blobs—strange other-worldly life-forms with unnatural colours and foul rot smells. These were not creatures of the sun but of death and decay. They spilled out from wood and on to the forest floor, their near-luminescent bodies glistening as they lurked in the darkness.

And there, right in the midst of all of the mess, stood the ugliest tree. Was it hardwood or evergreen? Living or dead? Its entire lower trunk seemed to be engulfed in the rot that spread out along most of its lower branches. And its crown was ragged and sparse with drooping branches edged with pale green-yellow needles. Fur did not like the look or feel or smell of the thing. He did not like it one bit.

"You are here!" called out the tree monstrosity. The voice was gruff and stern. "You are here," it repeated more slowly.

It's alive. It speaks. Fur was terrified. It was time to flee!

He heard the voice of white birch, calling him, then. "Little Fur, come back! You are in grave danger. There is trouble on the wing and it's coming fast!"

Fur had wandered too far. He realized that now, but too late. It was then that he felt the dull blows. Then he heard the buzz as small, dark creatures dropped from the skies. For a moment he was two places at once. But then he regained his true senses as his mind returned to his bodies in white birch. His dream voyage was over. He was back. He was under attack!

☼

Auja had followed Fur on his jaunt. It was easy what with that mosquito hawk leading the way. She had felt little Fur's giddiness as he gave chase through the trees and his alarm when he saw the giant rollers. She knew all about those hideous machines. They were the worst possible kind and they were gathering for an assault.

Auja had felt little Fur's terror when he had come upon the old swamp tree and could not bear her friend's distress any longer. She was about to reveal herself and send Fur some comforting words when she heard the white birch's alarm call.

Her senses raced back through the forest web to the birch and Fur's colony. What she saw made her lose all hope. She had this terrible sinking feeling. It was as if the soil had been stripped away, and her body was sliding into the earth. Why had she let Fur wander so far?

Runes

Fur had not heard the white birch calling soon enough. He knew he would suffer. They were big, ugly, hairy beasts. "Filthy swift flies!" he cried out.[60] There was a hoard of them buzzing around his colony—circling, landing, probing and laying. Some were leaving, others were joining in. They were all after the same thing on this fine spring day—crawlers.

Fur had seen swift flies before, but this kind was new on the scene this season. Auja had warned him about its sneaking ways. It would lay eggs on a crawler—near the head where they could not be chewed off. Slimy maggots would hatch and gnaw their way into flesh.

"Look through my leaves," cried the white birch. "They're laying eggs on you!"

Fur could see the smooth white droplets. He could feel them. "Help me!" he screamed in terror. The buzz grew louder as more and more flies joined the assault.

Fur's courage surprised him then. Instead of freezing with fear, he calmed himself, marshaled his crawlers and faced his foe head on. He tried the old trick from his early days—soft parts in and hard parts out, like the muskoxen of Big White. The swift flies did not seem to care. They attacked with even greater fury.

Next he tried to swat them away with his crawler limbs. "Heave, ho, heave ho, swing your heads to and fro," he sang out.

He focused on a single fly as it swooped in from above. He timed his response, striking out with three crawlers as his foe came within reach. Thud. His hard heads rammed into a soft underbelly. The fly was knocked out of the sky. Fur watched as its body fell to the forest floor.

Here comes more. He swung again. Smack. He knocked another from the air. *That's better, now for the others.* He looked for the next incoming fly. He saw something far worse. It made his crawlers freeze and go limp.

Birds. I'm a fool. His swinging and thrashing had attracted a pair of pine siskins. They joined the melee and started to gorge.

Fur felt searing pain as the birds began to rip him apart. He panicked. Some crawlers let go of white birch and fell. Some rushed blindly back and forth, knocking others to the ground as they struggled to escape. And some kept swinging their heads as if this could stop the avian assault. The agile birds picked them off with ease.

So this is death, Fur thought as he began to fade. In his final moments he looked up and saw a great orange ball in the sky. Flames swirled out from its edges and engulfed the deep blue. It was the sun. And it was getting bigger and bigger. Or maybe he was drawing nearer? He was! Awe overcame his fear and pain. He was going back to where he had begun.

Fur heard music as he drifted to the sun. It began with a simple beat that followed the sun's dancing flames. Then more intricate pulses and rhythms appeared. And a voice joined in harmony and sang a sweet melody. It was calling him back to the earth and breathing life into his shattered self. It was so beautiful, so soothing and … familiar. Hold on there, he knew that voice. He was sure of it. He could barely muster the strength to ask. "Is that you, white birch?"

"Yes," she replied.

"Are the birds gone?" he asked in a weak voice.

"Yes, they are gone. Now it is time for you to awaken. You must gather the survivors and rebuild your colony."

"I don't have the strength. Good-bye."

"Nonsense, this is no time for good-byes. We won't let you go. I'll help, but so must you."

No easy way out. Fur was going to have to face this. The pain returned. His crawlers were scattered on white birch and the ground beneath her. He tried to rein them in. He could not overcome their instinct to flee. Fur had lost control of his limbs.

Good thing white birch was there to help. Fur could smell her chemical tricks. She spat scent of leaf juice into the air. She lined silk trails with enticing aromas. No living caterpillars could resist. The survivors began to return and regroup.

It took a good while before Fur was finally whole again. He lay huddled up on birch's trunk, his bodies heaving as he struggled for breath. He checked his surviving crawlers. *Much worse than the roller. Seventy-three more phantoms to haunt me.* He blacked out.

☼

"Get up! Hurry, you're still in grave danger!" It was birch, shouting and shaking her branches at Fur.

Fur came to. It was still morning. He had not been unconscious for long. He flexed his crawlers. The pain was fresh and hot. "It hurts. I can't move," he said.

"You're going to have to! You're covered in swift fly eggs," said white birch.

Fur saw the bright white globules on the heads of his crawlers. He would lose another fifty strong once they hatched.

"Yes, I see them," said Fur.

"Good. Now you'll have to get rid of them," replied white birch.

"Get rid of them? How? Those crawlers are lost to me now. I'm weak and tired. Maybe I'll stay here for a while and wait for my bodies to sprout wings. I'm sorry things didn't work out like you planned."

"Hey! Come on! Pull yourself together. You can save yourself. Your crawlers must chew off the eggs—and quickly too, before they hatch!"

That was easier said than done. There was the walking, feeding and—as coined by Auja—even the muskoxen formation that Fur used for defence. There was harmony to such crawler arrangements. He did not have to think twice.

But gnawing eggs from one's heads? There was no formation for that. That demanded coordination, dexterity and fine control. Each crawler would need specific direction. Some must hold still while others grappled with an enemy stuck fast. And each egg might call for a different tact.

Fur tried and tried without success. It was work enough not to faint from the pain as his horde of new phantoms stung with fresh venom. It took him until noon before he managed to dislodge one. Not good enough. The eggs were near hatching. He could feel the maggots scraping against their egg shells trying to get at his flesh. He would have to try harder.

Off went two more, while the sun was high in the sky, and then another ten as the shadows grew long. And so it went as he worked faster and faster. Fly eggs once grasped were no match for his jaws.

"Pugh. Disgusting! Maggot flesh!" he said as he spat out the last egg.

"Well done!" said white birch.

Fur was exhausted. His wounds throbbed as he gasped for air. "Who are you?" he asked the tree, between pants.

"White birch of course."

"I know that. You're not the first birch I've tasted. But you're special. You saved my life!"

"That was nothing really," she replied.

"What do you mean nothing? What about the music and dancing ball of fire? How'd you do that?"

"I'm an artist," the birch replied. "I arrange and compose. I used the sun because it is dear to you. Then I added forest song."

"Well, you're a great artist."

"Thank you!" she replied. Her leaves rustled and shimmered as she spoke. "And you've not seen my best. I'm especially fond of flowers. My friends call me Gardener Birch. I couldn't be in a better place for it, really."

Little Fur saw nothing beyond a few spring blossoms. There was no music or sparkling sun fire.

Clearly, Gardener Birch saw more. "The ephemeral blooms are first to arrive under the old hardwood stand," she said to Fur pointing to a maple wood with one of her thin drooping branches. "Our newest display now shows in the evergreen glade. Look, woolly blue violet, rose-purple gaywing, goldthread and bunchberry in white," she said, now pointing to a small meadow surrounded by dark green. "And on bare rock our columbine grows. It lures the hummingbird adding dashes of red and green to the show. In summer and fall the trailside flowers are spectacular. There's so much variety.[61] What a medium for the artist to explore!"

Fur had little interest in the flowers. *Can't eat 'em, so why bother?* This flower tending was not necessary for life. His was short and harsh. He had no time to stop and smell daisies, never mind devote the seasons to floral displays.

"Does it help you feed and grow?" Fur asked the birch.

"What 'it'?"

"The gardening and flower gazing."

"No, not really."

"Then why bother?"

"Why bother?" Fur could feel the birch's leaves shudder. Her voice was stern. "Well, that's quite the question," Gardener Birch said. "Why do anything at all? It pleases me and others as well. It helps our spirits grow." Her leaf shudders turned to branch shaking while she spoke.

"I might ask you the same," she continued. "Why bother? Why have you wandered so far from home?"

"I'm only trying to stay alive."

"That's it? It's all about you? Don't you feel part of something bigger?"

"Yes, of course, Auja and the forest. I'm trying to help as best I can."

"Yes, you are." Her leaves and branches now lay quietly about her. Her voice was calm. "And you've fared much better than the others."

"What others?" Fur asked.

"Do you think you're the first of your kind?"

"Yes!"

"Did Wandering Oak, our little Auja Stigandr,[62] not tell you?"

Stigandr? What's that? Fur wondered. "No, never!" he replied.

"Well, you're not going any further today. Relax, I'll tell you a story."

Fur was relieved. He would not begin crawling until tomorrow. But he could not relax. If there were others like him, he had to know now.

"Let's see," said Gardener Birch. "A long time ago, the explorers came to a place they called Markland[63] on our far eastern shores."

"Auja told me about explorers, and the Wendat, and the beavers too," Fur said.

"No. Not that time. This happened earlier—a thousand years ago—before the hewmen age of greed."

Gardener Birch continued with her tale. "These explorers[64] were met by first peoples.[65] There was fighting and killing, of course. But not all meetings went that way. Both peoples revered the forests. Trees were more than leaf and wood to them.

"It is said that one warm autumn night in the dark shield forests, there was a Gathering of explorers, first people and trees. It was a sublime moment when all spirits joined to revel in the glory of becoming. Mammals danced while trees swayed to the rhythms of the forest in spring.

"The explorers told of their mysterious language—their whispered secrets. It was a new way of speaking to their kin and their ancestors across space and time. It was a language of symbols etched in stone. The symbols were called Runes."

Runes! The forest web was abuzz with talk of the Runes. Auja had called Fur 'Runes' when they first met. Many trees called him by that name even now. What did he have to do with a thousand-year-old legend or scratched stones, for that matter? "Please tell me more," he pleaded.

"In the spring of that year long ago, there had been a great crawler outbreak," replied the birch. "The aspen and birch from that legendary Gathering were laden with the eggs of your kind. Soon after in that exact same place we discovered the most remarkable crawlers. They spoke to us!"

"Amazing!" cried little Fur. "How'd it happen? Where'd they come from? Surely they didn't pop out of nowhere."

There was a long pause. Gardener Birch seemed distracted. Fur could hear her whispering to someone else but could not tell what she said.

"We had such hope then," the birch finally replied.

Why won't she answer me? Fur wondered.

Gardener Birch continued. "We had found a new ally and a way to communicate that would help to preserve our tree way. The talking crawlers would be *our* Runes. We would reach out across the rivers and lakes, the prairies and mountains, the deserts and barrens. We would speak to the lonely island trees!"

"What happened to them?" Fur spoke loud and clear to make sure she heard his question this time. He felt a sudden hope then. Maybe he need not be so lonely. Maybe there were others like him to be found?

"It was not meant to be—at least not then," the birch replied. "Most were killed by crawler plague. A few survived and changed into moths. But none of their offspring survived."

Fur let out a sigh as his hope disappeared. There *had* been others, but they were no more.

"Then a terrible fire swept over that land," Gardener Birch continued, "and much of what we knew was lost. We waited and watched year after year for a return of your kind. As the seasons passed and the truths faded to rumour, our hope gradually failed us. And then ..." White Birch paused.

"What? What happened next?" asked Fur.

"You know the rest. Auja found you. And right in the nick of time. What good fortune!"

"Runes, eh? So I'm not so special after all."

"Of course you are," replied the birch in a more playful tone. "Who else would abandon all good sense to chase mosquito hawks across the land?"

"Sorry. I must be more careful. But that was really something. Did you see me fly through broadleaf, needle and root? That darner was no match for me!"

"Yes, indeed. I was impressed. You've come a long way, but then you've only begun. You wait and see. What if you could *be* every-where! What if you and all the trees could join together as one? There would be no need for chasing, now would there?"

"Is it possible?" asked Fur.

"We'll see, but that's not for you yet. Now it's time to eat and rest. You've suffered heavy losses. The next stage of your long crawl will be difficult. You will leave the easy treks along the man-trail and go north through the bush. There will be no bright forest edges to ease your way. You must crawl through the cone and spire of dark green. Sleep well tonight, my little one."

Dark Green Grove

There was no way forward except through hemlock and balsam fir. Fur asked if he could backtrack and circle round through the broadleaves. The trees said no. He pleaded for more rest. He was weak from his loss and could not continue. The trees would not budge. They kept grumbling about their precious farm. They said it would take days to reach it and there was not enough time.

Fur could hear the alarm in their voices. He could not escape the fear and gloom that flooded the forest web, and so he finally relented. He would have to go meet the evergreens.

It was sunny and warm and dry—a perfect morning for trekking. Yet the thought of that cold, dark forest kept him from leaving Gardener Birch. Every time he agreed to start, his crawler feet seemed unwilling to comply. Odd, after being crushed by rollers, drowned by rainstorms and preyed upon by swift flies and siskins, he found the dark green so terrifying.

Of course, all those other things had come at him by surprise. It was something different entirely to walk willingly into a dark and dreadful place. Though Fur had traveled through evergreens using Southcrop Vision, he had never actually walked upon one with his own feet.

"Hello, Fur. What's the trouble here?" said Auja, who had come to see him off. "I know you've suffered, but it's time to begin."

"Remember the last time I tried the straight path?" Fur replied. "That roller nearly finished me for good. I'd prefer to try the long way this time." He was stalling, though he knew there was no choice.

"The long way's no good this time. The safest route lies ahead," replied Auja.

They both paused to take a good look at the woods.

☼

Auja loved the conifer stands and often wandered to this grove to enjoy the scenery. There was the striking symmetry of balsam fir cone and spire rising up and out from slender, smooth grey. She sampled the pungent fragrance of needle and resin. It warmed her thoughts. "Each perfect fir peak points the way to a star." That's what her mother used to whisper at night.

In sharp contrast stood the much larger hemlock with rich, green feathers drooping over graceful boughs and big, ragged crowns growing out from rusty brown. Here and there on the forest floor the elegant wood fern burst out from darkness. "Magnificent," Auja said.

☼

Little Fur hated the look of the wood. It was a murky scene of shadow and gloom, an eerie place where the sun was not welcome. "You sure you want me to go in there?" he asked with a quaking voice.

"Yes, come on now. It's the only way," replied Auja.

Fur was not so easily convinced. "You must be kidding. All I see is a dangerous trek across sharp pointy needles and oozing bark blisters. There's no food. How can I crawl in that? Dark forest is no place for crawlers."

"Actually, their needles are not sharp, they're flat," Auja replied. "I'd imagine they'd feel quite nice for walking on. There are others that think so too. Look there!"

From the white birch's boughs, Fur borrowed hemlock's needles to have a better look around. He saw caterpillars, but they were much different than his. They were hemlock loopers. He could tell right away from their dark smooth skins and the odd way they looped their bodies to move.

"And look there, on balsam fir," said Auja.

These ones were bigger than loopers. Their hairless bodies showed dark brown with light spots. They were busy building cozy nests of silk and shoot tips.

"Budworms," Fur said. He remembered all that Auja taught him.

"Yes, very good. If they can do it, why can't you?" asked Auja.

Fur had to agree. They weren't much to look at. They did not even have fur coats like his crawlers but looked comfortable none the less. "You're right," he replied. "If those hairless little caterpillars can handle the damp shade, then so can I."

"There's the spirit. Now let's go. The conifers will guide you. You'll get used to them. And I'll be with you all the way," said Auja.

Fur began cautiously. He did not move all his crawlers at once but first sent his strongest to make the crossing. They laid plenty of silk along the way and doubled back to reinforce the trail with reassuring scents. Then they marched back again from broadleaf to needle with the others in tow. The whole colony finally came to rest on the evergreen trunk.

Fur was immediately greeted by the harsh and throaty but cheerful voice of a hemlock. The tree seemed very excited. Her soft, tiny needles, stroked Fur's feet as they rustled. "Hoi there, little one. Pleased that you've joined us! Welcome to our grove of dark green!" she said. "Though we can't hope to feed you, we are honoured to hold you in our needles and branches. Come, little one, we'll show you the way!"

"Actually, my name is Fur," he replied.

"Fur? Why, only the mammals wear fur."

"I know, I know."

"Very well, Fur it is," said the hemlock. Then he shouted out for all to hear. "The broadleaf Runes have arrived! Hail to the little one—the one who is many. Hail to little Fur!"

The other evergreens joined in the welcome with a ragged chorus of good will. "Here! Here! Welcome, welcome, little Fur!"

Fur's spirits were buoyed as he marched from tree to tree, but not for long. Auja had been wrong. Crawling along these foreign leaves and branches was not easy. His wounds ached in the cold, making every step smart as he lumbered his way through. The darkness of the grove and crude evergreen vision made it hard to see. True, the needles were not sharp, but their narrow shapes and small sizes made for difficult walking. He much preferred the breadth of broadleaves.

Fur had to keep close to hemlock's stems, as the needles could not bear his full weight, while balsam fir posed its own challenges. Its bark could be treacherously sticky in places while its harsh stench was overwhelming. After his first half day of torturous trekking, Fur was struggling.

"Hey, Auja," Fur called out to his friend. "I can't breathe in here." His crawlers gasped for air. "How do those loopers and budworms do it?" He waited impatiently for her reply.

"They belong here," Auja finally said. "I do apologize if I've misled. What's right for others may not be for you. That's what we mean by diversity. There are so very many kinds of forest caterpillars. Each has its own special way to harvest a patch of sun rays."

"What are you talking about?" Whenever Fur was hungry, he ate leaves not light. "Crawlers don't eat sunshine like plants."

"But they eat us trees and take the sun's energy stored in our leaves," Auja replied. "Each species has a unique way to get at it. You like broadleaves; loopers and budworms prefer needles.

"And it's not only the forest caterpillars that harvest sunlight. The creatures that eat you, they're after the same, and those that eat them take their share too. Others wait until you die before having their fill.[66] And so the sun's energy flows through the web of life, feeding all who have found their own means to reap it."

Auja knows everything, Fur is simple. "So what? Who cares?" Fur muttered. In fact, he did care—about anything to do with his cherished sun. But he was not getting any closer to it by crawling through this dark green mess. For once he was not in the mood for idle chat; he was having enough trouble breathing.

The upshot of Auja's little speech was that loopers and budworms were fine here and he was not. There was no quick fix for bad air and cold and this treacherous route. The sooner he got out, the better. He picked up the pace.

The husky voice of balsam fir called out suddenly, "Watch out, little one! I've got a bit of the canker rot. You'll get stuck if you're not careful!" It was the tree he was slogging across that had spoken.

Stuck in what? he wondered. It was then he noticed many of the fir trees had oozing sores along their lower limbs. This grove was sick. He wanted out *now*. But he was having trouble moving his feet. It had nothing to do with fear this time. The bark was sticky. *Got to keep clear of this gummy gunk.*

Too late. A part of him was already caught. It was eleven unlucky crawlers in the front of his column. He came to a halt and assembled his other crawlers.

He listened as the balsam fir scolded Auja. "Come now, Wandering Oak! You must take better care. You should have been watching instead of distracting little Fur!"

"I'm so sorry, little one," said the evergreen more kindly as she addressed Fur. "I tried to warn you!"

"How am I supposed to know what a canker rot is, eh?"

"It's a fungus that rots my—"

"Whatever," Fur interrupted "What am I to do now?"

"Can't you pull yourself out? Come on, give it a try."

He wiggled and writhed but that only got the crawlers more stuck. And now their furs were covered in sticky resin. The greater his effort, the more futile it became. He finally uttered the unthinkable. "I'll have to let them go and push on."

"Maybe it's for the best," replied the balsam fir. "Time is running out for us all, little one. You could drop them like hardwood leaves and carry on with your journey."

It was somehow fine if Fur said it. But coming from a tree it sounded callous and cold. His crawlers were not dead leaves to be cast away! They were very much alive.

Fur remembered the deadly fly eggs. He had rid himself of those monsters by making his body do extraordinary things. It took concentration and coordination. *My crawlers must work together.*

He had an idea. He stretched himself out in a long line up the trunk, above the fir tree's oozing sore. Each crawler grasped the rear of another using its forelegs. He was a thin furry snake. Then he did something he never imagined possible—something he knew caterpillars were not supposed to do—he actually walked backwards!

He found after several tries that if his bodies pulled together he could generate enough force to extract a stuck crawler. It took the rest of the afternoon, but by the end of it, all eleven were free.

Their feet were torn and carried a hard coating of balsam fir resin. Fur walked with a limp to his evening's roost in an aspen tree. As he hobbled along, his new lilt seemed to say, "Never give up, never give up, never give up."

For two more days, Fur slowly zigzagged from one broadleaf to the next across the great expanse of dark green. Finally by the third, the hardwoods grew more common again. He said farewell to his odd companions and left their dark needles behind. He was told he was soon to find a very important tree—a tree unlike any he had ever seen.

Seer Elm

Fur was making good time in this bright broadleaf forest of poplar and yellow birch. The food here was good and plentiful. It was a perfect place to moult. He stretched and stretched until his skins could not bear to stretch anymore. They ripped open. Fresh crawlers burst out wearing new fur coats once again.

Fur used Southcrop Vision and borrowed the surrounding leaves to take a good look at what he had become. He could not help but admire himself. No creature he had ever seen—no creature Auja had ever showed him—wore such brilliant blazes of blue.

Fur had reached his last crawler stage. Despite all he had been through, he was alive and felt his chances were beginning to look brighter. He still had close to one hundred crawlers and they were growing more powerful by the day. What he had lost in numbers he made up for in size. The pain of his old wounds had diminished.

Fur took one last look at himself from his broadleaf vantage. He knew his striking blue could not last. This fifth stage marked the beginning of his end. The colony, having served its purpose, would soon split up. Each crawler would go its own way to find more leisurely pastures and a warm and cozy place to begin the big change. Keeping them together would only get harder and harder.

☼

Fur was excited. He was nearing the end of his third day in this pleasant woodland, and he was finally to meet the Seer. The Seer was no ordinary tree. She was a very old white elm, and according to Auja, that was special enough these days. But this tree was particularly special.

"The Seer is the wisest of trees. She's a distinguished scientist—an eminent empiricist and theoretician," Auja said.

"What's that supposed to mean," Fur asked.

"She's very smart. She has grand ideas about important things, then she samples bits of the world to check if she's right."

"And is she?"

"Almost always. In fact she has honed her talents to such a degree, that it's said she can predict the future!"

"Is that possible?" Fur asked.

"Maybe yes, and maybe no, but if anyone can, it's her," Auja replied. "She'll deny it and give her usual lines. 'Nothing's for sure. I predict—I forecast—but I don't see the future. It's all a matter of probabilities,' she'll say. No one listens. She's been right too many times."

Despite what had happened in the evergreen grove, Fur once again had been talking and not looking. The aspen tree shoot he was walking along suddenly ended and he almost banged into a massive trunk. It belonged to a very odd looking tree. He had never seen anything like it before. Could this be an elm?

"Are you the Seer?" he checked to make sure before leaving the aspen.

"Yes, I am," the elm replied. "I've been waiting for you. I cannot believe that you have made it this far. Success! Against all the odds, it has worked!"

"What's worked?" asked Fur as he moved onto the elm and began to crawl up towards her top branches.

"Well … er … um … I mean you of course. And the plan," she replied. "Perhaps there is some hope for us yet, though not likely. 'Better to expect the worst,' I always say. Then I will never be disappointed," she added in a gloomier tone.

Hmm. Not the most cheerful tree, thought Fur. Auja had warned him of this too. *Hope she tastes good.* He wanted to look for the positive.

Elm was a very large tree. Fur was trying to get to her upper branches where he expected the best views of the countryside. But given elm's height and zigzaggy twigs, he figured it would take a good while. So he turned and headed to her south-facing side, where he found a bright and comfortable place for a quick bite.

"It's nice to finally meet you," said Fur. He began to nibble on elm's green. He was wary at first. Her leaves were a little intimidating, with large toothy edges that reminded him of carnivore teeth. But their taste was alluring and he dug right in. They were not rich and hearty like oak—not sweet and juicy like cherry—not light and bracing like aspen—they were ... strong and a bit spicy and ... sad. Why would the elm taste sad? Maybe she was lonely?

"You're the first elm I've met. Where are your kin?" asked Fur.

"Look to the forest floor. See the young ones?"

"Yes, now that you mention it. Never noticed really. I don't go down much. Where are the grown-ups?" asked Fur.

"Well, that is another matter. They are mostly gone. The forests are littered with our dead. Look there," said the elm, as she pointed to three naked trees nearby with a shake of her leaves.

It struck Fur then as he made the connection. He had seen these lifeless forms before. The grey mottled bark with deep crisscrossed ridges was familiar. So too was the way branch and bough fanned out from the trunk. It reminded him of a bird's tail spread in display. But he had never seen such a tree fully dressed with leaves.

"I do know your kind. Is this land unfriendly to elms? Are you at the limits of your range?"

"Oh no. There was a time when we roamed deep into the cold Dark Forest—from the far eastern oceans, to the prairies in the west—and down to the rich south of the continent. We even grew in hewmen places, lining their trails, and softening their harsh dwellings with our finest canopies. But those days are past. We elm are in decline. We have been ravaged by disease."

"Like crawler plague?"

"No, a fungus[67] born by a bark beetle. It destroys our circulation. Our branches die and then so do we. It spread so fast. I lost all of my friends and family. Not since the Big Ice has there been such tree destruction. Even now it continues to kill. The days of the grand elm are through."

The sad taste of elm's leaves suddenly overwhelmed all else. Fur could clearly feel her pain. His crawlers trembled and shook as the leaves of elm quaked with emotion.

"That's horrible. I'm so sorry. How did it happen?" asked Fur.

"It is a new disease. We were not prepared. Men brought it from over the eastern seas," said the elm.

"You're a wise, elder tree. Can't you find a cure?"

"That is not what I do. There are others who work on that problem. My concern is not with one species but with all. I study the whole."

"The whole of what?" Fur asked.

"The whole of the earth. The living sphere. I study how everything fits together."

"How do you manage that?"

I gather information. I measure, monitor, sample and survey—land, water, sky and trees," said the Seer.

"So does Auja and the other trees as well. She's told me about the spring count, and the summer and fall counts too," replied Fur.

"And what do you think all the counting's for?" asked the elm.

"Don't know, really."

"For me, and for other scientists in Southcrop. I gather up the numbers and all the little pieces and put them together again."

"Why?" asked Fur.

"To observe. To try to understand how things work. To try to predict what will happen next."

"What things?" asked Fur.

"Everything! Water, rock, air—in fact, the whole of the world and all life that dwells upon it. And to understand the whole, you can't pick it apart. You don't always get answers by looking closer and closer. Sometimes you have to stand back to see most clearly."

"So what do you see, Seer Elm?" asked Fur.

"These days? Trouble, to put it simply. Have you not heard? The forests are in grave danger."

"Why? Does it have to do with your farm by Oak River? Is the secret of Southcrop Vision in danger?" Fur knew he was heading for this farm and wanted to know more.

"We trees have more to worry about than our Riverside Farm," said the Seer. "Its plight is only a symptom of a much worse disease."

"What disease? Do you mean crawler plague?" Fur asked.

"No! Enough with your plague. You must think bigger than yourself, bigger even than this forest, little one. I mean the plague of hewmen that is sweeping our earth. No forest is beyond their reach. There are sad trees everywhere!" With those words, elm's leaves stood up stiff and straight and prickled Fur with their teethy edges.

"How do you know that, eh?" asked little Fur. "I thought Southcrop was cut off from the rest of the world."

"Not entirely. We have our ways. The winds tell us and so do the birds."

"You talk to the birds? What do you trees need me for, eh? Let the birds carry your treasure across the river," said Fur.

"That would be convenient. Then I wouldn't have to waste my time explaining everything to you," the Seer replied. "Sadly, we can't speak to the birds, though they tell us much nonetheless."

"Tell without speaking? How's that?" Fur asked.

"We read their signs—their Bird Sign. The birds fly far. They're our remote sensors. We watch where they go and everything they do. We count them as they fly south and when they come back and then again when they have young each year. We sample their nests, their droppings and leftovers and even the smells on their bodies. We check who gets sick and who lives and dies, which species flourish and which ones decline. In short, we read the birds."

"O.K. I get it, I get it." said Fur.

Fur was well aware of the problems Southcrop trees faced—their shrinking borders, their isolation, their long struggle with the hewmen and their machines. But now it sounded like the whole world was in peril. "Tell me, Seer Elm, what's happening beyond Southcrop?"

"Even now as we speak, our final refuge—the great northern Dark Forest—is beginning to fall while southern trees surrender to men's sprawl. The hewmen are grabbing up the land from all living things to fuel their expansion. There is no place left for the rest of us. They are causing a great extinction—perhaps the worst of all time. We are losing our biodiversity, the key to our survival. How will we cope with the change that will come?"

"What change?"

"A terrible change. A sudden and permanent change—a catastrophe! The hewmen force will cause it," Seer Elm replied.

That did not help. Other than some bad weather and a few chilly nights, Fur had not noticed too much out of the ordinary. And the warm sun always returned. "Where?" he asked.

"Everywhere! On land and sea and in the skies. The hewmen force has already pushed the earth into very new territory. Take the air, for example. It is unlike anything we have experienced in over a half million years.

"We see the warning signs," the Seer continued. "The earth is warming, the weather more extreme and storms more violent. The rhythms of the forest have grown strange and wild. Even insect outbreaks are more severe." Seer Elm shook her branches as if to add further weight to her claim, while Fur hung on tight as he was swung to and fro. "I see air and sea currents shifting. I see rising waters, cold and ice, and searing heat and drought."

"Can't you do something to stop it?" Fur asked.

"We do what we can—what trees have always done. We preserve the familiar. We make the world liveable for life."

"How's that work, eh?" he asked.

"Well … how should I put it, maybe not entirely accurate, but … we breathe," said the Seer.

Fur was not impressed. "Yeah, so what? So do I."

"Well, you can thank us for that!"

"Thank you trees?" Fur wondered whether it was only Seer Elm or all the scientists that thought themselves so important.

"In part—and the rest of green plants and algae in the seas," said the tree.[68] "There is a special gas[69] that we pull from the air to build our bodies and store the sun's energy. We breathe this gas to extract the sixth element."[70]

"What's a sixth element?" asked Fur.

"The foundation of life. The stuff you and I are made of. We take the element and charge it with sunlight, then pass it along throughout the food web. But it all begins with us. We are the producers and providers."

O.K., so maybe Fur was impressed. "Incredible!" he said.

"Yes, we are," said Seer Elm. "And we do even more. We strive to keep the earth's atmosphere in order so that life will flourish."

Some trees were haughty for good reason. If true, then not only did trees rule over the earth but the skies as well. With such powers, surely they could take care of their big problems. "So where's the trouble then, eh?" asked Fur.

"Well now," replied the Seer, "this special gas while up in the air helps to trap the sun's heat and keep the earth warm."

"Warm's good, isn't it?" asked Fur.

"In moderation, yes," Seer Elm replied. "And by pulling the gas from the air, we try to keep the earth's temperature just right for everyone. But without our efforts, the gas builds up and the earth gets too hot. It's this warming that will help cause the terrible change of which I speak. And once it happens, there'll be no turning back—not ever. A very different world awaits us—a harsh and precarious world."

Seer Elm spoke as if this were certain. "But you said you trees tend the air? Can't you fix it for us?" asked Fur hopefully.

"There are not enough of us anymore," replied the elm. "The hewmen are destroying the balance we strive to maintain. With one hand they cut us down. With the other they dump more of the gas back into the air. It comes from their burning. They burn to make energy, to fuel their contraptions, and to clear the lands. The hewmen are born to burn. We trees can no longer overcome their force. They are making the world unliveable for us trees. So we can no longer help keep it liveable for others. It's a vicious circle."[71] The elm's voice had been growing louder all the while she spoke.

What a sad and angry tree, thought Fur. The elm's leaves had turned even more bitter to taste. And her branches were shaking more vigorously than before.

"Ignorant hewmen—arrogant hewmen—your heads have grown too large!" Seer Elm cried. "Your greed has brought us all to the precipice. It will push us over the edge and down to our darkest age."[72]

Fur tried to cool her down. If he did not he figured he would soon be thrown to the ground, what with all her shaking and swinging and swaying about. "Won't there be trees standing long after the hewmen are gone?"

That seemed to help. The Seer was thankfully still again and her voice grew calm. "Oh, probably—a few here and there, only bits and fragments, nothing more. True, we have survived other great changes in the past. But not without great suffering and harm. We will forget our tree way and lose all we strive for. We are nothing without each other, my little one.

"But now that you have made it this far, perhaps you will survive the journey," the elm continued. "And if you succeed it will be you and your line that will help to preserve our tree way. It will be you Runes that will help to carry Southcrop Vision to our refuge in Dark Forest."

"So you too believe in the legend of Runes?" asked Fur.

"It is no legend. It happened. But this time is different."

"How so?"

"You are alive and so we have hope. We have one last chance to succeed where others failed long ago. Now, go rest. A formidable challenge awaits you. The next stage of your journey will be the most dangerous. We will not be able to guide you so easily this time. You must pass through the blind forest."

That evening little Fur did try to rest. He knew he would have to move on tomorrow at dawn. But sleep did not come easily. The whispering 'others' were becoming much harder to ignore. They were pushing their way into his mind. This time they seemed more frantic. He could make out a few words. They were saying good-bye. Why? And why did they sound so scared? He felt their fear. It swept through him and then lingered, sapping his strength and will. *What's a blind forest?* he wondered.

Blind Forest

Little Fur was near the end of another day's travel, having left Seer Elm behind that morning. He came upon a towering pine that stood on the edge of a bluff. Having now become more familiar with evergreens he climbed to her very tip top. There was no food here, but he wanted a view. And what he saw puzzled him to no end.

A strange valley lay before him. For as far as he could see there were trees stripped bare of all their leaves. Here and there, like dark green dots on the landscape, lone conifers stood out, with leafy needle-crowns in an endless barrens of branch and wood. Whatever could have happened?

The friendly hemlocks had shown him scenes like this from the cold season during his stay in their grove. But it was a warm evening, and there was obviously no white cover of snow.

Beyond the valley was a wetland that eventually met the banks of Oak River. He was getting closer to his final stop at Riverside Farm. The thought did not help him now. He knew he would have to cross through the valley to get there, but how?

He had no answer so turned his attention to food. He climbed down from white pine and onto a tattered old oak that stood nearby. He ate his fill—and then some—as usual. The taste and smell of her reminded him of Auja.

"Good evening, Fur!" It was Auja of course, right on cue, stopping by to clear up his confusion. The sound of her voice was such a comfort. "What do you think? Now that valley's quite a sight, to be sure."

"What happened down there? Fur asked. "Looks as if most of the trees are dead! What terrible creatures would do this?" he asked.

"Why you, of course. Your outbreak hit hardest down there. On your own you don't look so scary, but in numbers your kind becomes a powerful force that shapes the forests and all its inhabitants."

Fur was amazed. He had seen patches of leafless trees throughout his trek, and there were plenty of crawlers wherever he went. Even so, he never imagined that all their leaf chomping could do such a thing.

He borrowed what tree leaves he could find and zoomed down the valley slope for a closer look. He did not get far before his Southcrop Vision faded and his way was blocked. He returned in an instant, feeling quite puzzled.

"You blame us, but I didn't see a single crawler down there. Where'd they all go?" His question went unanswered. "I did see plenty of crows though." He could still see the black specks in the distance and hear their 'caw-caw-caw'-ing.

"Yes, the birds are gathering," Auja replied. "And there are cuckoos and orioles and many others as well. Your juicy pupae are a treat for all."

"Oh dear. I've had enough of birds already," he said as he recalled his deadly encounter with the pine siskins. The more he learned about the valley, the less he wanted to go in. "And what happened to my Southcrop Vision? I couldn't get very far."

"No, of course not," Auja replied. "The trees have no leaves. They're mostly all blind."

"Then I'll be blind too if I go down in there!"

"Have you forgotten your own eyes? You'll have to use all your senses to make your way through. And remember too, the leafless trees won't be able to speak."

"So I'll be all alone?" asked Fur.

"Not entirely," replied Auja. "We'll help. We are in root contact with the valley trees. And we have leafy sentinels waiting for you. We've worked out a plan. We hope each day will begin and end with you in the boughs of a tree flushed with green."

"I do enjoy the company of evergreens," said Fur. The neighbouring pine he had used for a view bent over ever so slightly and shook a mighty limb at Fur in appreciation.

"But what about food?" Fur asked Auja as he considered the pine's needles. "Sure doesn't look to be much down there."

"You'll find none," said Auja. "The only broad leaves are red maple. You can't eat them. It's not done."

"What about other scraps? Surely there are tasty bits somewhere."

"No! It's too dangerous."

Fur had only just finished gorging on oak. But at the prospect of no food, he began nibbling nervously on another leaf. "Why?"

"Plague! You're looking at the centre of your outbreak. It started here first and will end here first as well. From our vantage, you can see the beginning of your decline. In another year or so tent caterpillars will vanish from this place. It's already started. Where do you think all the crawlers have gone?"

Fur did not want to believe it. "The big change! All the crawlers must be curled up and hidden away. They're growing wings even as we speak!"

"Not so. They're all dead—mostly from plague," replied Auja.

"Please, no—say it isn't so!" Fur stopped eating. He was overcome with dread as his crawlers all slumped flat against the oak's leaves and twigs. He would never survive in that valley of death, nor would any of his kind. Would the tent caterpillar go the way of the white elm? "Are the days of the crawlers over and done?" he asked.

"Don't worry, my friend," Auja replied, "only for a short while. You will surely rise again—and then fall and rise some more."

"What the ... what are you talking about?"

"Your cycle."

"What cycle?"

"Your population cycle," Auja said. "Your rhythm, your beat, your dance. The way your numbers rise and fall at such a regular pace—like waves crashing on the shores of Lake Attigouatan. It happens every ten years or so. Up you come and then down you go. It's the most remarkable thing. I noticed it first with you tent caterpillars and then found others who do the same.

"Remember the hemlock looper?" Auja continued. "They dance to a beat and so do the spruce budworm. They dance more slowly. It takes thirty years for them to come and go. And it's not only you moths.

"The birds and mammals in Dark Forest and Big White dance too; lemming, vole, mouse and shrew, ptarmigan and grouse, squirrel and hare—along with their predators—owl and fox, coyote and lynx—weasel, ermine, fisher and marten.

"Their pulses of energy cascade through life's web. Each has its own rhythm but all are connected. There is synchrony and harmony! It's all part of the music of our biosphere. It's been playing since the very beginnings of life. You've heard some of it already, haven't you?" Auja asked.

"When?"

"Remember Gardener Birch?"

"Oh, yes," Fur replied. "So that's what that was. Her music saved me!"

"Indeed," said Auja. "She's a master composer. But where do you think she gathered all the parts? What was it you saw while she sang?"

"The sun!" Fur replied. "That's where the music was coming from."

"Yes. The sun creates the music of life. Some like Gardener Birch are able to sift through, filter out the noise and arrange it for us."

Fur remembered then what the Seer Elm had said. '*The earth is warming, the weather more extreme and storms more violent. The rhythms of the forest have grown strange and wild.*' "The music is changing, isn't it?" Fur asked Auja.

"Yes, it is."

"It's because of the hewmen."

"Yes."

"Their force is now stronger than the sun's," Fur said.

"Hah! The sun will burn bright long after hewmen are gone," said Auja.

"But by then it'll be too late for you," Fur said. "It may be too late for all of treekind."

"You're right. You've been talking to Seer Elm. So you understand why we need you. Our Southcrop way, our Southcrop Vision must reach our final refuge, far to the north, at the top of the world in Dark Forest! Only from Dark Forest can we survive. It's up to you, my friend."

Fur could almost feel the crushing weight of tree hope upon his bodies.

"You'll have to go into that valley for us, Fur," Auja said, "and make your way through without food. So, it's time to eat."

"I've eaten my fill."

"Not full enough. Eat until you're stuffed to bursting, and then eat some more. Then please try to get a good night's rest!" said Auja finally.

The eating part was easy for Fur, as always, but the sleeping part was not. There were too many voices, too much debate that carried on through the night, and it all concerned him. The problem, of course, was plague. The entire valley was contaminated. All the naked tree bark, from bole to twig tip was covered with the tiny virus pieces. Each one was sitting and waiting for caterpillar flesh.

Finally, little Fur drifted off and started to dream. He wished he could moult and begin anew. He stretched as he slept and then stretched some more in the hopes there might be fresh crawlers within him. He wanted big, strong and fast crawlers that could leap and bound over the blind forest. Or maybe crawlers that could spin long sticky strands of silk would be fine. If he could squirt the silk far so it stuck to the sun, then he would swing over the blind forest and never once touch wood.

His bodies kept stretching until they burst wide open. But instead of new crawlers, millions of tiny beasts streamed forth. These were hard and sharp and cruel. They joined a mighty torrent and flooded the forests killing all tent caterpillars in their path. Little Fur's bodies had been stolen by others. He had become the crawler plague.

Fur woke up shaking in terror the next morning. Why should he continue? He blocked out all the tree voices and struggled with the question even as the sky brightened.

Did he want to reach the sun? Yes, that was his dream. If he stayed here it might come true—and soon! And he could rest and eat, and bask for a while before his big change. The thought was so tantalizing.

Yet chasing his dream meant the end. Before growing wings and flying to the sun, his crawlers would scatter, then spin their cocoons and drift off to sleep. They might survive, but he would die. It would all be over for Fur—all done for the little one.

Why wish for such a thing? The sun had given him life. Yet ever since birth it had been calling him back. To what? Was he so ready to leave this place? Was his life not short enough? Maybe he could hang on a little longer and help others before rushing off to the void.

Then again, if he tried to help by crawling into that dreadful valley, he would surely die of plague. Would that not be far worse? What good could that do for anyone?

He heard Auja's voice calling to him. "Fur, it's almost time to go."

Go how? Which way? Fur was still quivering with fear from his dream. "How will I know the right path?" he asked Auja.

"We'll tell you, of course. Did I not say? There are green trees in the valley who will guide you."

"How will I find these trees then, eh?"

"Each evening we'll let you know the next day's route."

Fur was not convinced. "But what of the plague? How am I to crawl clear? I can't see it. If what you've told me is true, it must be almost everywhere."

"You may not be able to see it. But we can. We'll mark your trails. We'll even wash them clean of virus," Auja said.

"With what?"

"Our sap. Keep your eyes open for trickles and drips and wet patches of bark. They will mark the safe paths," Auja replied.

"You mean you can control the flow of your sap?"

"Of course! We're trees after all. Now time for one last nibble my friend, and then off you go!"

Little Fur did not nibble, he gulped—from fear rather than hunger. *Stay or go, stay or go?* he wondered. *Stay here and aim for the sun, or go crawl—for the earth and my dear tree friends?*

Sun Showers

Oh bother, I'm going to regret this, Fur thought as he began his journey through a row of aspen.

As long as there were leaves, the trees continued to pass him instructions. "Go northwest, keep the sun to your side and behind. Stay away from the tree trunks and the lowest branches. Head for the old beech—you'll know its smooth bark—then turn left to the sugar maple and straight on to the ash. From there, take a little hop over to the largetooth aspen." Then their words began to mingle together, until there were really no words at all, "And onward to the ironwoodmapleblackcherrytreefirgrove ..."

It sounded more like whispering wind by the time Fur had reached the last green tree. Auja joined him to say good-bye.

"How am I to remember?" asked Fur. "I couldn't understand a thing."

"The messages we've sent are now part of you. You'll know the way," she replied.

"Are you sure?"

Auja's long pause made Fur even more uncomfortable. *Stay or go? Stay or go?* He had lingering doubts.

"Legend says it's so. You'll remember," she replied. "Now make sure to keep your eyes peeled for our markers. And whatever happens, don't be tempted by the silk trails of your kind. They'll be laden with plague. And listen carefully, Fur!"

"Yeah?"

"Are you paying attention?"

"Yes."

"Beware of the wind! If the slightest breeze begins to blow, don't linger. You must find shelter under branch or bough! Is that clear?"

"Yes, yes, all right already!"

"Good-bye and good luck, my friend," said Auja.

The last of the leaves disappeared and the forest grew quiet as Fur crawled down toward the valley. It was an eerie silence. He realized then how accustomed he had become to the chatter and hum of the 'others'. He stopped and gathered his crawlers in close, unsure of his next move.

"Hello, anyone out there? Which way do I go?" he asked, knowing full well that no one could hear him. *Darned trees*, he thought. This was not working. He would have to turn back.

He had to admit, he felt such relief at that thought. His mind grew calm as his bodies let go of his tension and fear. That was when the instructions appeared. They unravelled inside and pointed the way. The trees had been right. He could remember!

But they did not tell which tree limbs to follow. One false move and he might crawl right through plague. It would spread from his feet to his fur and in through his many mouths. Then he would catch the disease and his horrible dream would come true. Where were his friends to guide him now?

"There!" he cried as he saw a tiny dark patch of bark. Then he noticed others beyond it. From vein, stalk and scar the trees sweat out their wet trail markers. His friends were with him. There would be no turning back.

Fur swallowed the fear that welled up inside him again and started on his way. He soon realized that the trekking would not be easy. There were no broad green, leafy paths rolled out for his feet. It was all stick and twig, branch and bough.

Throughout that day Fur saw signs of other crawlers—moulted skins, heavy silk trails and old carcasses—but no living ones were to be found. The tent caterpillars had wiped the forest clean of all green and then had completely disappeared. He hoped he might see telltale signs of the big change—the slumbering pupae snug in their cocoons. He saw none and was beginning to feel that Auja was right after all. *All dead, every single one.*

There was something else strange about this forest. When Fur had first set out, there was a brisk wind blowing, but now down in the valley not a breeze stirred the air. It was unnaturally calm. Auja had been so concerned about wind; could it be the trees were making it so? By now it would not surprise him. Just when he was thinking he had these trees all figured out, they would reveal some new power that seemed like pure magic.

Fur's target this day was a small stand of balsam fir which he reached at sunset.

Good company at last, he thought as he heard the pleasant evergreen voices.

"Welcome, little one! Come relax in our branches, little Fur. We are so pleased you've made it this far. Rest with us and we'll plan tomorrow's route." Little Fur spent that first night hungry but in good spirits.

The next day was much like the last: more green-tree hopping through the doldrums of the brown wooden valley. The conifers were his beacons and he spent much time with the grand white spruce, who cheered him with pleasing banter and shared their Southcrop Vision.

☼

By the end of his fourth day in the blind forest, Fur was starving. He had never gone so long without food. He knew this could not last. Exhaustion joined with his hunger to weigh him down and thwart his progress. He usually felt lucky to have so many feet. But now each one felt like a stone, which once thrown seemed too heavy to lift up from the tree bark.

Fur was plodding on, his heads hanging low, when he spotted light green up ahead. It was no dark-needled conifer. It was a beautiful broadleaf tree with a fully flushed crown. He picked up the pace.

Must have food. Keep eyes peeled. Follow sap markers. Stone feet be darned, he ran.

The tree was now close. He took a good look. Its bark was dark grey, ridged and flaky. Its square, toothy leaves were unmistakably maple, with light green tops and silver bottoms that looked welcoming—until Fur crawled upon them.

The smell of the foliage made him queasy. "Phew! That's disgusting. No food here," he said. It was a red maple. It was not meant for eating.[73]

The foul smelling tree replied, "You are right. No food for you. I am red maple and not for your kind. Normally I feel quite fortunate not having to deal with your crawler chomping. But am I ever glad to see you. Now, rest your weary feet. Oh, I wish I could do more. I wish I had something for you to eat."

"No worries," replied Fur, not wanting to offend. He was lying of course. He worried plenty. How could he go on with no food?

"Tonight at least, you can enjoy the pure brilliance of broadleaf vision and wander far from this valley," the maple said. "You are nearing the last stage of your journey. Once across this valley, you will travel to the wetlands and Riverside Farm. There you will rest before crossing to Deep Sky."

"What's this farm all about, eh?" asked Fur, hoping this tree might reveal more than Auja and the Seer had. "Auja tells me it's nothing like the hewmen farms I've seen."

"You're right," replied the maple. "It is not of men. We trees have been farming ever since there were forests. We even taught hewmen how, though it's hard to believe. Their methods are so vulgar and their farms so drab. Ours are treasures and the one you are going to is the greatest in our land. If all goes well you will see it soon."

"Yes, about this treasured farm of yours. How do you grow Southcrop Visions there? How will I carry them to Deep Sky?" said Fur.

"Ask the Farmer," the red maple replied.

"Who's the Farmer?"

"Cross this valley and you will find out." The maple would reveal nothing more.

About as helpful as Auja and the Seer, Fur thought.

That night Fur was too exhausted for playful forays. There was only one thing he wanted to know. He used Southcrop Vision to find the closest tree with tasty leaves marked clear of all plague. And there it was, so close yet so far. It was a fine old basswood with those odd lopsided leaves, standing beyond the valley, beckoning to him. Was it too far to make in one day? Maybe, but he would sure give it a try.

After a sound sleep, a deep blue, cloudless sky greeted Fur at dawn. His crawlers hastened to leave, spurred on by a desire to reach food by nightfall. He was famished, but the sight of food, no matter how far, gave him energy to continue. He sped along and made good time, since he did not ever have to stop to eat. By noon he noticed a slight breeze in the air. He reached another red maple stand soon thereafter. The trees seemed sullen and anxious.

"Welcome, Fur. It is time for a break. The weather has turned and you must stay here."

Fur was not to be waylaid so easily. "What weather? Looks fine to me. It's a beautiful day. Why stop now?" he said as he continued to cross from one end of maple's crown to the other.

"Stop! Please! It is too windy."

"You call this wind? There's hardly a breeze. I can't stop. If I do it'll be for good. I must find food!"

"No. Please don't. Tragedy will befall you," cried a chorus of red maples.

Fur ignored their desperate pleas. "No way, I'm not stopping now. It's on to find supper." He crawled and crawled, not ever once looking back until he had left the crying red maples far behind.

☼

Auja was beside herself with grief. She did not have to hear the news. She watched it happen. A part of her died then from the shock—one of her lower limbs went cold and numb. It was only a matter of days before the leaves would shrivel and fall.

Wicked hewmen. Ghastly machines.

Southcrop Forest had lost another farm.

☼

As Fur entered a wood of aspen and oak, the wind kicked up and it began to rain. Odd, since there was not a cloud in the sky overhead. No matter, a few drops would not hurt. But with wind and rain came faint whispers. From chewed up remains of green stem and leaf vein, the trees called out to him. He could feel their fear. And now he could make out their words.

"Take cover, take cover," they said. Fur was at the tip of an oak branch considering his next move when he heard them. That was when Auja's warning came back to him. The wind was blowing. He had to find shelter. He made a dash for oak's trunk.

Fur was stretched thin as his crawlers ran two and three abreast. He was almost there. Then one of his crawlers, about half way down the line, stumbled and stopped to regain its footing. Others bumped into it from behind. There was a pileup. A large raindrop splattered the stalled group. The drop was thick and sticky and smelled foul.

That's no raindrop—it's raining plague.

Where had it come from? He looked up to the treetops and saw writhing fur. There were hoards of caterpillars wandering this way and that but going nowhere at all. He knew they were infected and were trying to escape the disease that consumed them. They were surrounded by limp and broken bodies. He watched, horrified, as the wandering dead crept aimlessly through a forest of hanging crawler corpses. It was almost as if the trees, having lost all their leaves, sprouted putrid cadavers instead.

Fur was now split into two parts, separated by a deadly wet strip of virus that coated tree bark. One part cowered in a huddle against oak's trunk. The other crawled to the ends of a twig to see if there was some way to escape. There was not—the twig tip touched nothing but sky.

Fur was still one—one little one, as the trees might say. It would take more than this slight distance to splinter his self. Yet he was hopelessly torn. He could not leap over the deadly wet bark to bring his bodies together. And even if he could, many of the crawlers stuck out on that branch were covered in plague. They would become infected. They would join the wandering dead above and turn to putrid sacks of virus. He struggled to control the panic that swept through him and froze him in two shivering masses.

Fur knew it was foolishness, but he had to try to save those stranded crawlers. Maybe not all were contaminated. He remembered the dark green grove and how he had freed his stuck caterpillars there. He still walked with a limp, and even now it spoke to him. *Never give up. Never give up.* Fur remembered how he had chewed those nasty eggs from his heads after the swift fly attack. That too had seemed impossible before he had tried.

But this time was different. There would be no comforting words from his dear friend, Auja—no Gardener Birch to save the day. He would have to get through this alone. He spotted a nearby twig that might be useful. If he pulled it down and over the wet bark, he could use it as a bridge and bring his parts together.

A sudden gust of wind shook the trees. Thousands of limp bodies began to sway. Many broke open. Then came another sun shower of death rain. Fur's stranded crawlers were hit again and again by oozing globs of plague. He shook and twisted them as if this could rid him of the goo. But he knew it was hopeless, so he let go. One by one his crawler bodies jumped from the oak branch in a last desperate attempt to escape the disease. Fur could hear the soft thuds from below as they crashed to the ground.

Each falling crawler let loose a memory that flashed and then faded as Fur's mind splintered.

> *Sunshine,*
> *tasty oak buds,*
> *filthy swift flies,*
> *roller crush,*
> *dark green grove,*
> *little one,*
> *Wandering Oak,*
> *evergreen needles,*
> *Gardener Birch song,*
> *Sad Seer Elm,*
> *silver lines,*
> *phantom pain,*
> *Fur,*
> *Auja …*

He was no longer afraid. He would give in and let all his parts scatter. A few crawlers formed a line and crawled up oak's trunk. Others turned round and walked down to her lower branches. His last renegade thoughts flickered by.

> *Green flash,*
> *zoom and dart,*
> *buzz,*
> *wing blur,*
> *hover,*
> *mosquito hawk.*

These thoughts were not memories. The green darner had arrived! The darner flew straight at Fur and then stopped right in front, holding its body motionless while it beat its wings furiously. It almost seemed to be waiting for him. Fur called to his wandering crawlers that were within his reach, then pulled and tugged and yanked them back in. They huddled in close to confront this final foe.

"Aha! I've met you before. Were you taunting me there? Are you up for another race?" Fur called out half-crazed to the dragonfly.

The winged giant hovered there for but an instant more, then darted off. Fur watched as it flew north toward the Oak River wetlands. How he longed for Southcrop Vision so he could follow that darner out of this desolate valley for one last good chase.

Not going to happen, he thought. He would have to use his own feet this time. His choices were simple, the answer was easy. If he gave up now he would die alone in this horrible place. He would fail Southcrop Forest and never reach the sun. If he could only manage to pull himself together again, he could go after that green darner and finish what he had begun.

Stay or go, stay or go—for Auja and the forests … and me?

Better to give this quest one last try. He would not let it end in this plague trap. No death-walks to those hanging corpses for him. "Wait up, green darner, I'm coming after you!"

The wind had died down and the foul rain had stopped for the moment. It was time to make a dash for it. Fur's choice had been simple. Following through was not. Most of his bodies were gone and he was near starving to death.

He tried to run, but his crawlers kept tripping over his new phantom limbs and the pain of his losses sapped what little strength he had. *Forty-seven more to haunt me.*

Some crawlers straggled, some tried to wander off to find food, while some would not budge until pushed by others. His bodies were no longer under his control. *Fine time to fall apart*, he thought as he finally began to hobble clumsily along in a ragged column.

Which way do I go? The forest was coated in oozing plague. It stank. Hoards of noisy flies zoomed through the air in search of crawler flesh. There were no evergreen or red maple guides here to find him safe paths and warn him of danger.

Where are the markers? Where's my trail? Then he spotted the sign way up in the crown of the oak he was lumbering through. It was a dark stain of wet dripping down from twig to branch, then bough and trunk. *Thank you, sweet sap.* He raced up toward it. Why was it leading him up to the tree tops? There was only death and disease that way.

Wet bark is wet bark—must be a safe path. It was not until he had almost reached the stain that his suspicions were roused. His front crawlers suddenly pulled up short. Another pileup of tangled crawlers ensued.

The dark patch was not quite right. It was wet but had a purplish hue. And it smelled off. Then he saw something that made him shrink in horror. All his piled up crawlers fell backwards. There was a dead caterpillar up above the wet patch. A flesh fly had alighted upon it. The fly unfurled its tongue and probed the limp body which then tore fully open. Its insides began to drip, down onto the branch right in front of him.

This was no sap marker dropped by friends. It was a mark of death. It was plague! Fur backed away from the stream of virus that oozed its way along the branch toward him. He would have to be more careful. There were traps everywhere. He spotted another dark stain and crawled toward it most cautiously. There was no purple tinge and no foul smells. It was clear and clean and had a sweet and pleasant aroma. He followed it and spotted another.

He kept going in his slow and cautious way, inspecting each marker before moving along. Finally he began to see green. Little by little, the leaves were returning. He had crossed the valley. The forest was no longer blind, nor deaf, for that matter.

"Food—where is it?!" Fur cried.

"You must wait," came the reply. "You know that. Not until the old basswood."

Yes, of course he knew, but he felt bitter disappointment nonetheless. And the feeling did not go away. In fact, he grew more and more gloomy the further he crawled. It was not only the hunger that troubled him.

The tree voices were back, but they were filled with grief. No one seemed willing to speak to Fur. Something was very wrong. He called for Auja. She was always cheerful. And good cheer was exactly what he needed. He had been ravaged in that valley and was more phantom than flesh by now. For the first time ever, Auja did not come. Had something terrible happened to her?

By nightfall, Fur arrived at the basswood. No welcome awaited—no friendly hellos. He ate in silence. The leaves were clean but tasted bitter and sad like Seer Elm's had. Fur longed for Auja's company more than ever. He called and called for her long into the night until he finally succumbed to exhaustion and fell into a deep sleep.

Farmer Tamarack

Fur woke up crying for Auja. She did not reply. Using Southcrop Vision, he travelled back to the old glade. There she was, same as usual, though her leaves hung limp and wilted on one of her large limbs.

"Hey, Auja, come on, wake up," he said. "Are you hurt?"

"No, I'm fine."

"Are you angry with me?"

"No, not angry at all. It's so good to hear from you."

Auja's cheerfulness seemed forced and out of place amongst the grief that hung over the forest.

"What's going on? I made it through the blind forest! Shouldn't you all be thrilled?"

"Yes, well done."

"Why all the sad trees?"

"We've lost another farm," Auja replied in a whisper.

Fur's mind began to race. Which farm? The one that held the secret to Southcrop Vision? What would be left to carry across Oak River?

"Is my quest over?" he asked Auja. For an instant he was relieved. Maybe now he could stop and rest—for good. But then he felt bad for having such thoughts.

He let the passion of the forest sweep through him. The pain and sorrow became his too. There would be no more wandering free through the leafy canopy. No more visits to Auja and the glade. No more dragonfly chasing. No more sharing!

This was about more than Southcrop Vision. Southcrop Forest was doomed without its farms. The forest web would fail and each and every tree would be left to die alone. That is what the forest was telling little Fur—not with words but with emotions, which he felt more painfully than ever before. Had the trees' worst nightmare come to pass?

"No, your quest is not over," Auja replied. "It was our southern gem, the farm at Rock Edge that fell to the hewmen."

Fur's relief felt real this time. His bodies tensed up and his crawlers shook with excitement. It was not too late.

"It's hard to feel lucky after such a catastrophe," said Auja, "but I suppose that's exactly what we are. Your quest is more important now than ever before. But you must make haste before the hewmen trample Riverside Farm as well!"

☼

For three days Fur crept through some of the most difficult terrain he had yet encountered. It was not only water that got in his way now. There was sparse forest and bare rock. Sometimes he had to crawl to the ground and cross the hot pink of granite in mid-day sun. It singed his feet.

And something had changed in the forest as well. Many of the trees were less helpful than before. They seemed cold and listless—as if they had given up. He longed for those early days full of hope.

There was a new sound that kept Fur on edge. He heard it most days and it got louder as he drew closer to Oak River. There was something about it that reminded him of rollers. He asked the trees and they sent him pictures. It was a roller indeed, but more massive than any he had seen. It roared and thundered and shook the ground as it rolled along silver lines.

For three nights Fur rested and listened. The chorus of the 'others' that swept over and through him grew louder and louder as he drew close to the river. After the fourth night and a heavy morning shower, Fur woke to bright blue. The dripping wildflowers and greenery bent the sun's rays back up to the sky. The brilliant flashes dazzled him as he crawled.

By early afternoon, Fur reached a bluff of rock, blanketed with lichens. There was something strangely familiar about this place. He crawled beyond the bluff's edge and down through red oak. *Hmm ... hemlock grove to one side, cedar-lined clearing to the other—I know I've been here before.*

But there was no time for sightseeing. He was supposed to reach the Farmer by day's end. So he kept on crawling through aspen and cherry, black ash and birch, then finally willow and alder. He tried to stop for brief nibbles along the way but each time was spurred on by his leafy hosts.

"Hurry up! You can come back for food later. Now you must go see the Farmer."

"Who's the Farmer?" he had asked more than once.

The answer was always the same. "You'll know soon enough," the trees would reply.

Well, Farmer or not, he was getting close to his evening roost. He crawled around a large rock outcrop and came upon a vast wetland. Beyond it he could see Oak River. He was drawing near to the end of his journey at last. But he also saw something, off in the distance, which made him shudder. They were rollers—big, ugly, fearsome rollers. He had seen these before, but where? He turned his gaze from the ghastly machines. That is when he noticed a most unusual tree. It too was familiar. He was sure he had been here before. He looked the tree over more carefully. At first he was not sure if it was dead or alive. It was covered all over in mushroom rot. But then he saw green amongst its sickly foliage.

"Aha! So you live after all," Fur said. "And if you're a tree, then you're the ugliest I've ever seen." He checked his bearings. He was on course. He crawled across an alder thicket toward the tree. It stood in drenched soil, surrounded by a multitude of shining yellow beacons[74] that looked like slimy mushrooms with tops that brightly glowed.

Maybe they were put there to ward off intruders? If so, they worked. He was scared. *Must be some mistake—I'm going the wrong way.* Fur's crawlers turned around and he began to retreat.

The tree creaked and groaned, "You are here!"

Fur knew that voice. It was the monster that had spoken to him that fateful day when he first chased the green darner using Southcrop Vision. Now he was back in this terrible place and facing this horrible tree. And he did not like it any better in the flesh.

But after looking more closely, it did not seem as scary. It was tall and slender with a pleasing straight trunk and reddish-brown, scaly bark. Its drooping branches were covered in clusters of soft feathery needles. It was no monster. It was a graceful tree in decline.

"Are you dying?" he asked, feeling sorry for her.

"Yes," replied the tree. Her voice was brusque but friendly in tone.

"Are you deciduous or conifer?"

"I'm both," she replied.[75]

"What … I mean who are you?"

"I'm Farmer Tamarack, and you are Fur, of course. I'm very pleased to meet you. It's remarkable that you've made it this far. Ha! Ha!" the voice boomed as the Farmer chuckled. Fur was pleased to finally meet a cheerful tree once again.

"There's one prediction the Seer got wrong," the Farmer said. "Of course she'd be the first to admit—nothing in life is for certain. That's what makes life worth living."

"Hey! That's what Auja's mother used to say," said Fur.

"Yes, and so here you are against all the odds. Beyond that clearing are the silver lines that join us with Deep Sky. Now let me explain—"

"Food. Where's food?" Fur interrupted. The trees had told him he was not to stop to eat until he found the Farmer. Here was the Farmer, and now his thoughts turned to his hunger.

"Well, I know of some fine broadleaves, but they're not so close by and you'd have to backtrack. You can nibble on me if you like," said the tamarack.

"What? I don't eat needle leaves," Fur said.

"Give 'em a try. They're soft and tasty."

So Fur did. They were awful. He would have to find better and soon.

"I hope you like 'em. I've done the best I could," said the Farmer.

"Not bad for a needle bearer," Fur said. Then, worried he might have offended the tree, added, "I'm honoured to eat you, Farmer Tamarack."

"And I'm honoured to host you for your brief stay here at Southcrop," the Farmer replied.

"Southcrop? I never left. I was born and raised in this land. I'm Fur of Southcrop."

"Yes, you are indeed. But what does Southcrop mean to you?"

"It's the place we all live. It's a southern outcrop of the rocky plateau."

"Yes—double meanings. It's also the name for the crops we grow here at Riverside Farm."

"What farm? Where is it, eh?" Fur asked.

"It never stays put for long. It moves all the time—every few centuries or so—to wherever the conditions are right. Lately it's been right here," Farmer Tamarack replied.

Fur's thoughts returned to the ghastly machines nearby. "So why don't you move it?"

"Believe me, we're trying. But we can't outrun the hewmen and their machines. They've come so quickly. They could flatten this place in a matter of days. So we must hurry. Hurry, hurry, little one!"

Hurry to what? he wondered. Fur looked around and saw nothing much more than a bunch of trees in various stages of decay. There were still-upright ones and leaning ones and ones that had already lay down. Some were almost fresh and whole, while others looked liked they had been swallowed up by the forest floor. Whether only a bit sick, half dead or mostly gone, all were turning back to the soils.

"Where are your crops?" Fur asked the Farmer.

"Look around. What do you see?"

"Not much but death and rot."

"Yes, that's it. Death and rot—the decomposers—the fungal realm! Take a good look. The fungi are marvels of nature."

Fur gazed full round while he chomped on tamarack's harsh, sour needles. For the first time in his life, he trained his sights on that other-worldly kingdom. On aspens and sugar maples he saw crusts, shelves, wedges and caps—and bright, slimy colours.[76] The firs had a yellow jelly. So too did the alders, though theirs was black.[77]

Fur looked down to the forest floor. There were lovely flocks of bright white pinwheels amongst the leaf litter, and here and there smaller troops of tan funnels.[78] Each fallen log was decorated with its own shapes and colours and textures. Some wore blue-greens.[79] Others wore blankets of brown caps and yellow cups. Many were studded with large pale pinks and clusters of bright orange.[80] The more closely he looked, the more he saw.

"Wow, there's so many kinds, all in one place!" Fur said.

"Yes. That's Southcrop for you. And this is only the beginning. As the season unfolds, there'll be much more to see. The late summer displays are spectacular!"

Fur was impressed but certainly did not share the Farmer's love for these bizarre life forms. "So what? Are you telling me you're running a mushroom farm here?"

"And slime molds. We mustn't forget them," replied the tamarack.

"And so ... what's special about that?" asked Fur.

"You're missing the point. Did Auja not tell you?"

"Tell me what—about mushrooms? Sure, she told me about them and even showed me some pictures. But ... to be honest, they never did much for me. They don't seem that important, what with all the other things going on in the forest."

"Not important? Now hold on there! How do you think we trees feed?"

"Sunshine, leaves and roots," Fur said.

"Yes, clever Fur, but not without our allies. We rely on an age-old partnership forged at the beginnings of treekind!"[81]

"You mean with those ... those ... things?" asked Fur.

"Well, some of them, yes. The puffball and fan, tooth and sea coral, toadstool, bolete, russula and morel—for starters."

"Allies, eh? How does that work?"

"We help each other. They bind with our roots. They bring us nutrients. We give them energy and the sixth element of life, exactly the way they like it."[82]

"So each tree has its own mushroom patch? But I don't remember finding mushrooms under every tree on my trek."

"Ha! You're not looking at the big picture. These beasts are too large to see all at once. They are mostly hidden underground. The mushrooms are only their fruiting bodies. They help them to spread and multiply. There's a whole other world beneath the forest floor. There lies a net of living fungal strands. They make up most of the earth's soils. Each net is an organism—a creature. They are amongst the largest living things on earth. Some are so very ancient, they have dwelled buried beneath for millennia!"

"So, you help to feed each other?" asked Fur. He was beginning to show more interest.

"Yes, but there's more. They are the foundation of our lives. They connect us all. They are our forest-wide web that allows us to speak. And now they have given us the greatest gift—Southcrop Vision! Someday, we hope it will be they who will bring all trees together as one!"

Fur could not contain his amazement. "What? Do you mean to say … the mushrooms make your forest web? The mushrooms make Southcrop Vision for you?"

"Yes, they do."

"No one else has these special mushrooms but you?"

"No, we think not."

"I can't believe it! Is there no end to the surprises?"

"No! Never—until you are no more! The world is a far more interesting place than you could ever imagine."

"Incredible!" Maybe fungi were not so boring after all. "How'd you ever find such helpful friends?" Fur wished he had a few pet mushrooms of his own to help him through rough times.

"We didn't find them, we made them so. It began eons ago, with a simple partnership. From there we used selection. We created their conditions. We trees control the soils, you know. So we took tiny steps, year after year and down through the ages. We chose those fungi with the right qualities and allowed them to grow and spread. Given enough time and effort—anything is possible. So there you have it," said the Farmer.

"Selection—of mushrooms? Incredible! What else do you farm?" Fur asked.

Farmer Tamarack grew silent. His reply came slowly. "There are so many wonders of nature that we trees have created. But there's no time for that. You must get back to your quest before it's too late."

"Yes, yes my quest. So what am I supposed to do?"

"You must gather up spores from several species. The time is right. You'll have to go down and walk amongst the mushrooms. In fact, you'll have to touch them. Their spores will stick to your hairy bodies."

"Say, what?" Fur's enthusiasm vanished suddenly. "That's your plan? I spend my whole life crawling here, through flies and foul weather, birds and plague, and now you want me to … to … rub up against some mushrooms?"

"Yes. As I said. Now's the perfect time. The morel fruiting season is nearing its end, while the boletes and russulas are starting theirs. And for this task we'll need more than one kind."

Soggy forest litter was no place for sun lovers. After all the horrors Fur had been through to get here, he knew it was a silly to be afraid. But his fear could not be denied.

The dark green grove had been bad enough, but this was much worse. He would have to climb down to the forest floor. Of course, he had done this before on his journey. But that was only to get from one tree to another, across warm rock and under bright sun. Wandering around on the dark, dank ground touching those gross slimy things would be something else entirely. Who knew what deadly creatures walked amongst them?

"Why would I put the mission in danger now?" asked Fur.

"This is your mission—to carry Southcrop to Deep Sky. You'll have to go," the Farmer replied.

"Why can't these spores blow over the river on their own, eh?"

"Good point. Our selection efforts have fine tuned these special fungi for vision. But when it comes to evolution, there are always trade-offs. The fungi that are most special to us are the ones that don't travel well on their own. And even if their spores did blow across, they wouldn't work. Southcrop requires the right fungal mix and exact conditions. There are many instructions you'll have to carry."

"And how am I to do that exactly? What other unnatural places will you have me crawl through to get them, eh?" asked Fur.

"No crawling needed for that. We've been passing you information all along your journey. Of course, you know this."

Of course, Fur did. He remembered the 'others'. Their whispering voices that brushed him like breezes had always been there. More and more lately, Fur had heard melodies too. "What about the music and song? I hear plenty of that too these days," he told the Farmer.

"We're sending you all that's dear to us—all that makes up our Southcrop way," replied the Farmer. "You must carry our memories across Oak River as well. From there we hope they'll reach Dark Forest someday."

"And if I do manage to get across, then what?" asked Fur.

"When the time is right, all we've stored inside you will be released."

Fur remembered how in the blind forest the trees' instructions had unravelled inside and had helped him find his way. But a few travel directions were one thing. The history of an entire forest, along with the intricate secrets of Southcrop Vision, was something else entirely. Fur was sceptical to say the least. "What time is that?" he asked.

"It is said this will happen when you change to moths."

"Who said?" Fur shot back.

"The trees who were there the last time Runes crawled the earth."

Those who are now long dead, Fur thought. "You sure put a lot of faith in a thousand-year-old myth," he said to the Farmer.

"There's more to that story than you know," Farmer Tamarack replied. "A small chance is better than none at all. Now, good night, my friend. We hope you'll give it a go tomorrow. It will be a very special day. If all goes well, it'll be your last in the land of Southcrop."

Harvest

"Wake up! Wake up! You've got to go now!" The sun was not even fully up. Fur thought he might get to sleep in, but he sensed panic in Farmer Tamarack's voice. He could stall no longer. He heard a loud rumbling from off in the distance. He knew what the Farmer feared. Rollers! He used his vision to zoom in for a closer look. They were waking up. They were starting to roll! They made such a racket and began to belch foul-smelling smoke. No wonder the Farmer was upset.

"O.K., Farmer Tamarack, let me have a quick nibble, and I'll be off on your mushroom walk."

"No time for food! It'll be too late."

Fur grabbed up one bunch of needles and stuffed a few of his crawler faces with the feathery tamarack fare. (He was getting used to the taste, and it wasn't half bad). Then he stopped to await the Farmer's direction.

"Now's the time, little one," said Farmer Tamarack. "The spores are ready to harvest. First, over there underneath the ferns, are some special morels nearing the end of their season. You can't miss them. They're the most grotesque looking by far."

Joy, thought Fur, *I'm beginning with the worst.*

"Do you see? They're cone shaped with honey comb caps and stalks like tree trunks."

"Yes, I see."

"And then on to the fresh boletes. Look there. They have brown, domed caps that sit on broad stalks. After that you can visit the russulas. They're easy to find. Look for rosy red and pinks, near the maples. Come back here once you're done. Then I'll show you the others. Now, off you go."

Fur gave no further protest. The colony began the slow march from canopy branch to lower bole. The leading caterpillars stopped above the damp ground. They swung their heads back and forth in unison, surveying the route ahead. This was not going to be fun at all.

He figured he would follow those bright yellow beacons that grew half-submerged in water. From up close he could see they glowed in the dark of the forest floor. They would light his way, but he would have to keep a safe distance, else his crawlers would drown. Down went little Fur to greet the forest floor and begin his Southcrop harvest.

Fur spent the early morning crawling from one choice patch of mushrooms to another, then back to Farmer Tamarack for directions. His caterpillars went along in single file and rubbed their hairy bodies against the fruits of death. Each choice mushroom had its turn wearing white-studded blue Fur.

It was cold and damp, but there were bright sun patches and tasty herbs here and there for the nibbling. Fur toiled all day while the sound of the rollers grew louder and louder, and their stench choked the air. By dusk his body was doused with fungal spores. They tingled and itched his skins to no end. Fur returned to Farmer Tamarack's branches, where he was given his final inspection.

"Good. Excellent in fact! You're ready!" said the Farmer. "Soon you'll be on your way. The silver lines are not far. You must get out of here before those roller monsters arrive. It's time to cross Oak River to Deep Sky."

Little Fur was overwhelmed by a sudden rush of voices from all the trees. There were words of warning and best wishes and songs of farewell. It was as if every single tree in Southcrop Forest was saying good-bye at the same time. He called for Auja. She came in an instant.

"Hello there, Fur," Auja said. "It's time for us to finally part ways. But please listen carefully; your quest is not over. There are plenty more dangers ahead. You must wait until the silver line roller has passed. Only then will it be safe to cross. Once on the bridge, you must resist the urge to stop and spin. You can't begin your change until you reach the trees on the other side. There'll be aspen and oak there for your final rest."

Fur thought back to his beginnings in Auja's branches. The great expanse of forest and sky had terrified him. He had come far and seen much since those days but felt small and vulnerable. He quivered with fear like a colony of first-instar hatchlings. He was heading into the unknown once again.

Auja had taught him everything. She made his world familiar. She was his dearest friend. Now he must say good-bye forever. Once over that bridge, he would leave this forest web and never see her again.

Fur heard an unnatural rumble from the other side of the wetland. He no longer needed Southcrop Vision. He could see trouble with his own eyes. *The rollers are coming. They'll trample the farm. Must get away from here.*

And what of his dear friend Auja? Once the farm was gone, she would face a slow and lonely death—a death only a tree could ever know.

Fur next heard the deafening screech of a machine. This one sounded different than the others he had just seen. There was a rhythm to its clatter as it drew nearer. He knew what it was—the silver line roller. For the first time he realized how close he was to those shiny strips of metal that lay buried in the scrub. Then he spotted it. What a monster! The roller stretched on and on—squealing and belching as it sped by. Its head crossed Oak River and reached Deep Sky well before he finally caught a glimpse of its tail.

"There's your cue," said Auja as the last of the groaning metal disappeared over the bridge. "Good-bye, little Fur. Once across the river and safely up a tree you'll be able to rest and grow your wings at last. Go on now. The sun awaits you on the other side."

"Goodbye Auja. I'll miss you so," said Fur.

☼

Auja's heart sank as Fur gathered himself and started on his way. She felt old and tired and lonely. Her friend would be dead and gone so soon while she would have to linger. Her boughs and branches weighed upon her. She watched through Farmer Tamarack's eyes as little Fur marched off in neat single file down twig, branch and bole, over leaf litter and pink rock, across old field and gravel, to wood tie and smooth silver, and beyond to Oak River and Deep Sky.

Part III:
Oak River Crossings

Little Hewmen

Fur crawled alongside the silver lines. He found the ground was uneven and littered with pebbles and weeds. He next tried crawling on top of the smooth, shiny strips. It was much easier and he made good time. He soon left the land behind as he crossed the hewmen bridge. Now there was only rushing water beneath. It roared as it passed, sending shivers through his crawlers. Their furry skins soon glistened with tiny river droplets.

If only Auja could see this. "Look at me! I go where no tree has ever been," he cried out loud (knowing that no one could possibly hear him). He took a quick breather halfway across the bridge. He liked this place. It felt safe. There were no enemies hunting crawlers out here. There were so many good places to hide. He could not help but notice all the dark crevices and gaps and cozy undersides on this hewmen structure.

Maybe he would stop for a quick nap—or maybe even a long one. Why stop at nap? Why not stop for good, spin a cozy bed and grow some wings? He was old enough. He need not crawl anymore. Here he would go safely to that long, deep slumber. Then he could fly straight to the sun.

Fur remembered Auja's warning. "Don't stop and spin," she had said. *Auja is gone. What does it matter?* He was ashamed for having such thoughts. *Auja's my friend. Helping her matters. Only a little bit further, then sleep.* Little Fur dragged himself up and began to crawl once again toward Deep Sky.

There was something tugging at the rear of his line. Then his line broke in two. A group of crawlers veered off the silver. Nineteen of his crawlers up and left. Fur tried to call them back. He tugged and pulled but they would not stop. He knew where they were going—to the underside of the bridge, where they would soon lay their silken beds and fall asleep.

Nineteen more phantom crawlers. He was not really wounded this time. No crawlers had been crushed or drowned or doused in plague or pierced or shredded or chewed. Yet his fury at having let so many slip away and the guilt at having let everyone down caused him pain nonetheless.

Fur limped on, once again weakened. But he did not have far to go. The north riverbank looked close and there was a stand of aspen and red oak as if sent there to greet him. And they had leaves. There would be fine dining today! He picked up the pace and crossed onto the far shore of Oak River. After all he had been through, it looked to be a simple trek to the trees. All seemed well. That was until he spotted the hewmen.

There were four to be exact—two big and two small. Maybe they were parents with young? The biggest was sleeping under a tree. Lazy mammal. The loud sounds and sudden motions of the little ones made him nervous. But he had to get to those trees and could wait no longer.

He crawled down from the metal and then across a line of littered stones. Next he crept through the tangle of wildflowers and herbs and found some flat bare rock where the walking was easy. His beloved trees were getting larger as he drew near. He kept his eyes on those two little hewmen who were bawling and squawking and running amok. "Play," Auja had called it. "It's what mammals do. It's a riot to watch!" she had told him.

Little Fur was not amused. He preferred the calm, slow movements of the big hewmen. These mini ones were way too erratic. They reminded him of the quirky hover flies that would freeze and dart and freeze in mid air—or the swarms of midges on high, that would bounce up and down in one special place and then bolt to another to bounce some more.

Fur had one last long stretch of bare rock to cross. Beyond it was a stand of aspen and one very large oak. *Forget the aspen. I want some oak.* He longed for the familiar—for strong, wide boughs and hearty leaves. He could almost taste and feel them now.

The babbling of the hewmen suddenly grew louder. They were coming close! Fur halted and did not stir. He knew he could easily be spotted out in the open on the light pink rock. His long snaking line of brilliant blue and white on black would surely be noticed.

☼

"Caterpillars! Look, Clare! Caterpillars in one straight line," said the young girl.

"Yeah right, Gabby. Is the smallest one named Madeleine?" quipped the older sister.

"I'm serious. Really. Look!" said Gabby as she pointed to the frozen line of crawlers.

"Cool! Let's catch them," Clare shouted. She ran to the boat and returned with a large glass jar in hand.

☼

Oh no. They've spotted me, Fur thought. His crawlers fled in every direction. It was no use. He was surrounded. Pink fleshy hands clutched and grabbed him. Large eyes gleamed from smooth, pudgy faces. White teeth jutted from cackling mouths.

He thrashed his bodies and swung his heads madly about. But the hewmen would not let him go. They poked and petted and squeezed his crawlers. It sickened him. He spat black bile. The hewmen squawked loudly but did not stop. Giant fingers lifted him one caterpillar at a time and placed him in a trap.

Fur could see outside, but when he rushed to escape he bounced off something smooth and hard. It was a see-through wall. He thought maybe he could walk around it. But after crawling twenty-three full circles he figured there was no way through. He then tried crawling up to the top but his heads butted against a hard, shiny cover. There was no escape. And it was getting hot. The hewmen had put the trap down in the open, far from any shade. It was a cloudless day. The sun beat down. The trap let in the hot rays but would not let them out. He would fry to death.

The little hewmen seemed indifferent to his plight. They sat there, jabbering and shrieking and peering at him through the trap. The clear walls twisted their faces into ugly grimaces.

Then, like fickle hover flies and midge swarms, the two dwarf hewmen zoomed off to hover elsewhere. They had abandoned him. The searing heat was unbearable. He paced round and round but knew it was futile. *Oh dear, what a horrible end.* He began to swoon.

☼

"Lunch is ready. Let's go, girls," mother called.

"Wait. We want to show you something!" said Gabby. She ran to retrieve the jar from its sunny spot.

"Look what I found—caterpillars," she said.

"We both found them," added Clare, who had joined Gabby for the show.

"No way! It was me!" Gabby said.

"All right, all right already!" said mother. "Let's have a look."

"What kind are they?" Clare asked.

"Tent caterpillars, I'd say. There are lots around here this year."

"Are tent caterpillars good caterpillars or bad caterpillars?" Gabby asked.

"Neither good nor bad. They just are," mother replied.

"Are what?"

"Tent caterpillars. Now come on, let 'em go. It's lunch time."

"But these ones are special," said Gabby.

"Why?" asked mum.

"Because they came from the other side. They crossed the bridge to see us. They want to be our pets."

"Spinning wild tales again, Gabby?"

"It's true! Mummy, mummy can we keep them? Can we take them in the boat with us and bring them home?"

"No, certainly not. Let them go! They'll die from the heat in there."

"No way! I want them," shouted Gabby. Tears began to roll down her face. "They're ours!" Clare cried.

Clare ran back to the boat and climbed in. "Then I want to go home now," she said. Her sulking was short lived. "Frogs!"

Gabby ran to see. With the children distracted, mother dumped the caterpillars out of the jar and onto the shady ground under the oak. Twelve had already gone limp. Their bodies lay twisted on the ground.

☼

Fur rallied his bodies for one fnal push and staggered up the oak trunk to safety. *Twelve more phantoms—only eighteen bodies left.* It was enough to break him apart for good. It would be so easy. Each of his crawlers wanted to run away. Each yearned for their own green leaf—first to nibble upon, and then to roll up in and go to sleep. Why not let them go? *No, not yet. One more thing to do.*

Contact

Once Fur had crawled to the safety of oak's lower crown, he stopped to have a quick look around. He saw nothing beyond what his own eyes could offer. There was no Southcrop Vision here. He was reminded of that rich and full life enjoyed by the Southcrop trees. And it was up to him to bring it to Deep Sky. There was no time to waste. He had to make contact right away.

"Hello there, riverside oak. I bring news and gifts from Southcrop," said Fur. There was no response. He tried again. "Hey oak! Can't you hear me?"

"What? Who is there?" asked the oak.

"It's me. Fur of Southcrop."

"Is this some kind of joke—a young sapling prank?"

"Look to the crawlers in your crown," Fur shouted as loud as he could.

"What crawlers? Oh bother, I thought I was rid of them for good. Now come on. Which sapling is playing games with me?"

Of course the oak would never have heard of Fur. He must be more clear. "I … I mean we are the Runes!" *No time to get into the I—we thing*, he thought. "We are the Runes of your legend. It's been a thousand years. Now we've returned!" He figured that would jog the old oak's memory.

It did take a while, but Fur could tell it was sinking in. The oak's leaves began to shake. Then her branches swayed and even some of her smaller boughs began to rock, while the rest of the forest remained quiet. It was as if the sky had sent a special wind gust for this riverside oak alone.

The tree finally spoke. "Runes you say? I cannot believe it! So the old legend is true!" Then the oak began to shout, "There are Runes amongst us! The Runes have returned!" Her voice was old and creaky but surprisingly strong. It thundered and echoed through the wood.

The response was immediate. First came the creaks and moans and the swinging and swaying. Then there was a rush of voices that hit Fur in waves. The voices grew louder and louder as more trees joined in. They even drowned out the birds. This forest was far bigger than Southcrop, that was for sure. Fur had never heard so many trees in his life. So many so quickly could mean only one thing. *Excellent—their farms must be O.K.*

"Hello, riverside oak. Hey! Are you still with me?" little Fur asked. Fur had lost oak's voice in the torrent of others. He did not have time to waste while the forest stood there and gawked at him.

"Yes, of course. I'm with you. Now tell me, how did you get here?" asked the tree.

"I came from Southcrop across the hewmen bridge."

"Southcrop? Why, that is incredible! We have not heard from those trees in years. What news do you bring from that fine southern forest?"

"I've got news a plenty," said little Fur. "I carry the voices of Southcrop inside me—Guide Oak, Sentinel Pine, Herald Aspen, Elder Maple, Seer Elm, Gardener Birch, Farmer Tamarack, Wandering Oak and many, many others as well. But that's not all. I bring a special gift!"

"Oh, how grand. A gift from across the river. Where is it?"

"On my fur."

"What fur? Only the mammals wear fur."

"Yeah, yeah, I know. Now look closely. What do you see?"

"Hmm ... Oh, I see spores—the spores of many fungi. Have you been rolling in mushrooms?"

"Yes, as a matter of fact. And for good reason. These are no ordinary spores. They are the seeds of Southcrop Vision, a magical harvest from Riverside Farm. It will change your world. Imagine if you could share all that you see and hear and smell, all that you sense and feel and remember. Think what that means. You could visit faraway places without ever moving. You could wander free without bounds. You could travel back in time through the memories of your elders."

"How could this be?"

"Well, you talk to each other through your forest web with no problems, eh? Now add a dash of these little seeds, and you'll be doing more than chatting. It's true. Believe me. I've seen it with my own eyes!"

"So what now?" cried the oak.

"You must care for them. Make them grow. You must get them back to your farms somehow. Only there will they thrive. Only there can they spread their magic through your forest web."

"But I'm no farmer. Can you tell me how?"

"No, all the answers are buried inside me. They won't come out until I change."

"Until you change? But that will take days and days. And there are so few of you." The leaves of the oak sagged as she spoke.

"You'll have to do what you can," said Fur.

"Yes, yes of course. If … I mean when your moths emerge, you'll tell us what to do. I will drop the leaves that carry your empty cocoons. The spores will be there. I'll call in the farmers and we'll go to work on the leaf litter and soils. Do not worry."

Fur was exhausted. He wanted to let go. He thought about what might happen next. Soon, each of his crawlers would be wrapped up snug in their silk cocoon and rolled leaf blankets. Then they would shrivel and harden. A half-moon later, little brown moths would pull themselves out into the light and take to the air.

Fur knew this was wishful thinking. He had gone from hundreds strong when first hatched to only eighteen at the end of his crawler days. That was not nearly enough to survive the final onslaught. A new hoard of enemies was waiting to kill him.

But there was nothing more Fur could do. "I'm finished. It's time to let go," he said. "Spin your silk beds, my crawlers. Cast off your old bodies and begin anew. Fly back to the sun if you can!"

Metamorphosis

Insides are churning. Body's melting. Wings. I can feel them sprouting. I can ... I can ... feel. I must be alive. Not possible. It's a dream. But how can I dream I'm alive if I'm dead?

☼

Pain. Ripping, tearing, chewing, biting, gnawing, stinging, burning. This is no dream. I'm being eaten alive.

Roller Attack

Auja watched little Fur crawl over the bridge. The last she saw, Fur's fuzzy line had stopped midway across Oak River. And all the while, the rumbling of the hewmen machines grew. They had rumbled before, but this time the sound was much louder and more ominous. Something terrible was about to happen. The rollers belched and growled at each other, then formed a line and began to move toward Riverside Farm from beyond the wetland. She heard the alarm calls spread throughout the forest.

There was a huge, ugly roller at the front of the pack with a long bent neck that bounced as the rolling feet moved along the bumpy ground. The ghastly beast stopped in front of an old black spruce and stretched out its neck until it towered right over spruce's top branches. Its head was tipped with wide round metal and sharp teeth that began to spin and whirr.[83] Then it lowered its twirling jaws. Metal touched wood.

Auja heard the cries and could feel the tree's pain through the forest web. She cursed the power of her Southcrop Vision but could not bear to look away. The roller pushed its neck down upon the wounded spruce. Wood splintered as the machine tore up the tree top. Even spruce's sturdy trunk could not withstand the force. The scream of the dying tree echoed through the forest. Auja could smell burning as the roller jaws flung bits and pieces of wood onto the forest floor. It shredded the entire spruce right down to its base and pushed its stump into the earth.

Auja saw a hewmen sitting inside the machine. It too bared its
pointy teeth in a ghastly grin. The machine would not stop. It rolled
right over the shredded tree remains and on to find more prey. She
knew that grand old spruce from her earliest days. Now it was gone!
And more would soon follow.

Behind the shredding roller was another long-necked monster
with clenching jaws. It stopped to grab up a huge bolder which it
flung to the side, flattening the ground as it advanced. It was clearing
a path for the rest of the pack—a metal menagerie more hideous than
anything nature could ever produce.

Auja felt the burning rage well up inside. It shot out through her
leaves and roots gaining strength as it joined with the fury of others.
She screamed and howled along with the rest of the forest. It sounded
like a vicious spring gale ripping through Southcrop, though the sky
was pure blue and the winds were calm.

Auja's sap churned as she shook and rattled her branches. But to
no avail. What could wood do against such false creatures? It was the
beginning of the end—the end of old friends—the end of Southcrop
Farm and Forest.

Auja watched the carnage spread. Try as she might, she was unable
to tear her gaze from the gruesome scene. The forest was being eaten
alive. Then the reach of her Southcrop Vision began to fail her as the
rollers trampled the trees of Riverside Farm. She could barely make
out the horrid shredding machine as it approached Farmer Tamarack
and then stopped, as if to savour its next kill. She felt no fear from the
Farmer—only sadness. Then the scene faded from view. "Good-bye,
Farmer Tamarack," she said.

Auja's Surprise

It was spring again, three years since little Fur had crossed over to Deep Sky—three years since the roller attack. Auja's senses were awakening once again as she stretched her limbs and burst her new buds. But nothing felt quite the same.

Most of Riverside Farm had been smothered with false-rock. Farmer Tamarack was dead. But a small part of her precious crops had escaped. And so the forest web—though much diminished—still pulsed with the life-force that sustained Southcrop trees.

The rollers had not retreated. After centuries of calm, what was left of Riverside was on the move again, and to more than one place—just to be safe and sure. That would take years. The hewmen had plenty of time yet to finish what they had begun.

For the moment the forest was peaceful. There were no more crawlers to sap Auja's strength. The tent caterpillar outbreak was over. New colonies were few, though she had attracted one lone moth who laid eggs on her last summer. The tiny crawlers had already hatched and were heading out for food.

Auja thought of Fur as she watched them march. She missed him so. Whatever had become of him? It was a fool's hope to imagine he might have succeeded. She was suddenly disturbed by a most unusual greeting.

"Hail, Auja Stigandr."

Only Auja's mother, long gone, and Gardener Birch knew her by that name. "Hello there, birch tree," Auja replied.

"I'm not your gardening friend. I bring greetings from Deep Sky," came the reply.

That was not the Gardener's voice. *Must be day dreaming again,* Auja thought.

"You're not dreaming."

Auja's leaves began to shake. She was scared. *Something's reading my mind, but who or what?*

Though once again she had not spoken out loud, the answer followed her thoughts.

"I'm little Fur," came the reply.

"Fur? Impossible!" Auja said.

"Not so. I'm little Fur and more."

"That's ridiculous. What impostor lurks that sees my thoughts and preys on my memories?"

"I'm no impostor! Fur is part of me. I'm he and me, both. I know his whole life from start to finish."

Could it be? Fur had been a simple and innocent creature. This voice sounded dark and wise.

"How have the black-winged damselflies fared lately?" asked the mysterious creature. "I'm hoping for a good flock by the creek this year."

Fur had loved those insects. Maybe it was him. Auja had to be sure. "What news do you bring back from the sun?" she asked.

"Nothing yet, I'm sorry to say. Turns out that fireball is a bit further than I thought, though I get closer and closer each year. I'll get there someday, I'm sure."

It was Fur. Who else would chase stars across the sky? "Little Fur?! What happened to you in Deep Sky?" asked Auja.

"An impatient tree. How refreshing! I've missed you, Auja. Now relax and I'll tell you a story," Fur replied.

Relax? How could she? Little Fur (or whatever he had become) was back. Auja was ecstatic. Her roots began to tingle. She wanted to shout and cheer. Fur had survived! But before spreading the news she had to hear more. "Oh yes, please do tell!" she said.

"All right then, here goes. The Rune crawlers survived the crossing to Deep Sky and took refuge with a riverbank oak," said the colony. "There most were wiped out by my enemies, but not all.[84] Two male and two female moths survived and mated, then laid their eggs in Deep Sky. The eggs hatched and it was then I discovered the most remarkable thing."

"What? What did you find?" Auja pleaded. She remembered like yesterday when it was Fur doing all the asking and she giving answers. But obviously times had changed and it made her feel uneasy.

"Little Fur did not die," the colony continued. "His moth bodies went back to the earth, but Fur himself passed on through and joined his young."

"How's that possible?" Auja asked.

"Don't know. Maybe through mother's egg yolk," replied Fur.

"This is amazing! It's wonderful! You have memory! You can speak to your kin across generations."

"But it wasn't supposed to turn out that way, was it?" asked Fur.

"What do you mean 'supposed to'?"

"You don't know the true legend of the Runes?"

"I believe it happened."

"And that's that, eh? You've never heard the full story? Incredible! Even the trees keep secrets."

"What secrets?"

The colony did not answer but continued. "I should've seen it before. You garden and farm the wildflowers and fungi. You tend the soils and even the earth's air. Why do you do it?"

"It's what we do. It's the tree way."

"Yes, the tree way, of course—the way to preserve your dominion over this planet! What else do you control? What more do you need? Have you found greed? Maybe you're not so different from hewmen?"

"Now hold on there." There was no insult worse than being likened to hewmen. Auja's temper flared and her leaves clattered. "What secrets have you uncovered?"

"Let's go back to the legend," replied Fur. "The story Gardener Birch once told Fur was true. The Runes first arose so long ago, after that famous Gathering of first peoples, explorers and trees."

"Yes, that's right," said Auja.

"But they didn't arrive like magic. It took another ten years after the Gathering before they appeared. It was ten years of furious work, but you succeeded, of course."

"I don't understand," said Auja.

"Listen and you will," Fur replied. "It was there at that Gathering a thousand years ago that you looked into the hearts and minds of the explorers. You saw what was to come and you were afraid. It was this seed of fear that spurred you on to your greatest work."

"What work?"

"Runes! For the first time in history you achieved the unthinkable. You created a sentient being. You trees made the Runes!"

All Auja's leaves stood up stiff and straight and perfectly still on their stalks despite the breeze that whipped through her glade. She thought maybe even her sap stopped flowing for that moment. Then she began to relax as a new understanding overwhelmed her surprise and confusion. *Makes perfect sense,* she thought. But how did little Fur fit in?

"So what happened to these Runes?" Auja asked.

"They were wiped out by plague. And then there was the fire where so much was lost. By the time you trees recovered, the explorers had left and you forgot your fear. And you also forgot how to make us Runes," Fur replied.

"So, what about you? You popped out of nowhere, a thousand years later. How? Why now?"

"Where there's a will, there's a way. You trees did it once, you could do it again. You only needed the right motivation. You've lost control over the earth. The planet now stands on the edge of catastrophe. Southcrop has been shrinking and your farms disappearing one by one over the years. You foresaw this end and knew the hewmen could never be stopped.

"Once more it was fear of these people that drove you. The further they forced you apart, the harder you struggled to remain together. And look what you discovered—Southcrop Vision! It had to be shared. You had new hope and a purpose. You relearned what you had forgotten. You created Runes anew. And ..." Fur stopped short.

"And what? What?!"

"This time I survived!"

Auja was having trouble digesting all this, and coming to terms with the new little Fur. Whatever happened to her fresh and simple sun-loving companion? Where was the old friend who loved nothing more than to loll about, nibbling on leaves, asking cute questions? Now it she whose questions sounded simple and quaint.

"I ... I had no idea!" Auja said "How'd you find all this out?"

"I've come a long way since I first crossed Oak River. And I've had much more time to learn. I no longer live day to day. Now, as you say, my life spans the generations. And my powers are ever growing. I can see into the minds of the trees. Not all the time, and not always so clearly, but I'm getting better and better."

Well, that explains a thing or two, thought Auja.

"Yes, I hope it does," replied the colony. "So I went on my own voyage of discovery. I searched and searched and finally found answers. The trees of Deep Sky know all about the Runes. They gave me the full story of your so-called legend. But I had to know for sure. So I returned to Southcrop to close the loop and find out exactly how I came to be."

"And now you know?" Auja was not quite willing to believe.

"Yes. I paid a visit to Guide Oak only yesterday. She wasn't pleased but confessed all. But then I already knew having seen her thoughts even before she spoke. It was quite the shock to finally know without doubt. And of course I was upset. I'm only another being's construction—like some hewmen machine."

"That's not the same. You're alive! You can do what you like. You have free will," Auja said.

"Yes, I suppose you're right. And I guess I'm grateful and happy in the end. If it weren't for you trees, there'd be no me."

Auja was less forgiving. She had been kept in the dark while Guide Oak had known all along. And there must have been other elders mixed up in this as well—sneaking around in the forest-web shadows beneath her roots. *How deep does this secret go?* she wondered. "And what about me?" she asked Fur. "Was it only luck that led Fur's mother to my branches four years ago?"

"Of course not. You were selected to raise her young—to feed little Fur and watch over him."

… *deeper than I could ever have imagined,* thought Auja. It made her feel foolish and used.

"Why me? What's so special about Wandering Oak?" she asked Fur.

"You have the right qualities, Auja Stigandr."

"And what are they?"

"Not sure, but they worked their magic on me. So please don't feel bad. I fulfilled your quest. And I didn't come back only to see Guide Oak. I also came back to see you," said Fur.

"Why?"

"I wanted to know if these secrets were your secrets too."

"No. I didn't know a thing," Auja said.

"I believe you. You were never very good at lying. Now that that's out of the way, I have to admit I came back to see my old friend and tell her a happier tale."

"Of what?" asked Auja.

"Of success! Fur's young colonies gave rise to moths that took to the air and had little ones like me. And these little ones in turn, gave rise to more moths that laid their eggs in far away places. Some headed northeast to the highlands and the Southern Envoy. Others went northwest around Lake Attigouatan towards the Kitchi-gami north shores. We are carriers and now we have memory, so whichever way, your voice will reach the fertile crescent of Dark Forest some-day—and maybe sooner than you think. Others headed south toward

Toronton and beyond to Lake Yenresh—or so that was the plan. But wherever we fly we always head straight for your farms."

"Why?" asked Auja.

"We bear gifts," replied Fur.

"What gifts?!" Auja asked, ever so hopeful.

"Spores! Your precious spores have survived! They reached the farms of Deep Sky where they've blossomed. Our moths are sowing them across the land. It will be a deep sky indeed, when trees everywhere can see and feel as one!"

Auja could barely contain herself. "Success!" she cried. "Our Southcrop Vision is spreading. Our Southcrop way will survive. We have a new ally!"

"Yes, an ally to nurture and protect but not to control," said Fur. "There can be no more secrets. I ask of you only one thing—help my line to survive. In return we will unite the trees."

"Hail to our new friend and ally!" Auja shouted out for all to hear.

"Here! Here! Hail to the Runes!" The trees responded in kind from all around.

"So tell me Fur … By the way, can I still call you Fur?"

"Of course. Like I said, I'm he. He's me. But of course, I'm not the only me. Fur colonies are spreading far and wide."

Oh no. Not that again. The "I'm we" was hard enough to fathom. She chuckled out loud before asking the question that was burning inside. "What news do you bring from across Oak River?"

"'Thank You!' of course, but that's not all. Be patient now and listen. This will take some time." Auja settled her leaves and waited eagerly for the story.

"The trees of Deep Sky have sent you a gift in return."

The End

Author's Endnotes

1 Monoecious: A plant that has both male and female organs.

2 Dark Forest: The Boreal forest.

3 Oak River: Severn River, Ontario, Canada. Part of the Trent-Severn Waterway that connects Georgian Bay to Lake Ontario by way of Lake Simcoe and the Kawartha Lakes to the east.

4 The fisher, *Martes pennanti* (Order: Carnivora), is a member of the weasel family, Mustelidae. Growing to almost a metre in length, it resembles a large black cat, but with a slenderer body and shorter limbs. It lives in dense forest where it eats small animals, birds and carrion.

Source:

Banfield, A.W.F. 1974. The Mammals of Canada. University of Toronto Press, Toronto, Ontario.

5 Hewmen: Name most commonly used by trees for the human species, *Homo sapiens* (Order: Primates, Family: Hominidae).

6 False-rock: Concrete, pavement, asphalt, etc.

7 Big Ice: The last ice age, ending in southern Ontario about 10,000 years ago.

8 The Forest Tent Caterpillar, *Malacosoma disstria* (Order: Lepidoptera; Family: Lasiocampidae). The newborns hatch early in spring and race against time to feed and complete their caterpillar life stage before their enemies can destroy them and their food leaves become too tough to eat.

About eight weeks after hatching from the egg, the caterpillars form silken cocoons. They turn into pupae and moths, which emerge about ten days later. Moths only live a few days. After mating, the females lay from 100 to 300 eggs together in one mass around small twigs. The eggs develop into caterpillars within a month, but the caterpillars do not emerge until the following spring.

9 Larvae (caterpillars) of moths and butterflies grow in stages, called instars. The forest tent caterpillar typically has five instars.

10 Big change: Metamorphosis. In many insects, including moths, wasps, flies and beetles, wings appear suddenly in the adults. This is called complete metamorphosis (holometabolous development) and consists of three main stages: larval, pupal and adult. At the end of the larval stage, young stop feeding and pupate. During pupation, adult structures (including wings) are developed and most larval structures are lost.

Source:

Barnes, R.D. 1980. Invertebrate Zoology. Saunders College, Philadelphia.

11 Rogue wasp: *Rogas malacosomatos* (Order: Hymenoptera, Family: Braconidae) is a common wasp that attacks caterpillars during their larval (caterpillar) stages. This wasp is a parasitoid—an insect that is free-living as an adult but completes larval development within the body of another insect, eventually killing it.

Adult *Rogas* usually infect second and third instar caterpillars with their offspring. The larval *Rogas* feeds on internal organs of the living host, slowing its growth and eventually killing it. *Rogas* then spins a cocoon inside the dead host and pupates. Eight to fourteen days later, the adult cuts a hole through the mummified caterpillar carcass and escapes.

Source:

Fitzgerald, T.D. 1995. Tent Caterpillars. Cornell University Press, Ithaca, New York.

12 Big White: Northern tundra.

13 The northern goshawk, *Accipiter gentilis* (Order: Falconiformes, Family: Accipitridae) is a bird of prey.

14 Floaters: The gypsy moth, *Lymantria dispar* (Order: Lepidoptera, Family: Lymantriidae). Trees call them floaters, since the newborns that hang from trees on silk threads are able to 'catch the wind' and float in the air to new locations.

15 This 'stink' bug, *Podisus maculiventris* (Order: Hemiptera, Family: Pentatomidae) is a generalist predator that over winters as an adult and hunts tent caterpillars early in the season. It injects prey with paralyzing saliva and feeds by sucking out liquefied body contents with its pointed beak.

Sources:

Fitzgerald, T.D. 1995. Tent Caterpillars. Cornell University Press, Ithaca, New York. Biological Control: A Guide to Natural Enemies in North America, Cornell University.

Weeden, C.R., A.M. Shelton and M.P. Hoffmann, Biological Control: A Guide to Natural Enemies in North America. Retrieved March 10, 2008, from http://www.nysaes.cornell.edu/ent/biocontrol/predators/podisus.html.

16 Technically speaking, little Fur had setae, not fur.

17 Forest tent caterpillars are univoltine, meaning they have one generation per year. Adults die the year before their young hatch.

18 Auja: Old Norse name meaning "good luck, fortune, gift, or happiness".

19 The Canadian Shield.

20 Source: Hosie, R.C. 1979. Native Trees of Canada, Eighth Edition. Fitzhenry & Whiteside Limited.

21 Windy Bay or Bay of Winds: Lake Couchiching, Ontario, Canada.

22 Ouentironk: Huron (Wendat) name for Lake Simcoe, Ontario.

23 Lake Attigouatan: Huron (Wendat) name for Georgian Bay, Ontario, Canada.

24 Lake Yenresh: Lake Erie. Yenresh was the Huron (Wendat) name for the peoples that lived by Lake Erie around the time of the fur trade. The trees named the lake after these peoples.

25 The Niagara Escarpment in Ontario is home to the oldest tree in Canada east of coastal British Columbia—a White Cedar, *Thuja occidentalis* (Arborvitae) (Order: Pinales, Family: Cupressaceae) dating from 952 AD.

Source:

Kelly, P.E. and D.W. Larson. 2001. A Review of the Niagara Escarpment Ancient Tree Atlas Project; 1998-2001. In: Leading Edge
2002: Focus on the Biosphere Reserve, Niagara Escarpment
Commission. Retrieved March 10, 2008, from http://
www.escarpment.org/education/conference/zeroone/index.php.

26 Big Falls: Niagara Falls, Ontario, Canada and New York state,
U.S.A.

27 Man-trail: Road or highway.

28 River Divide: The St. Lawrence Seaway.

29 Bird Sign: Some trees could tell of events from afar by carefully
observing birds.

30 Kitchi-gami: Ojibwa (Anishinabek) name for Lake Superior,
located in Canada and the U.S.A.

31 False-light: Light from human sources.

32 Deep Sky is also home to the Torrance Barrens—Dark Sky
Reserve, where many humans go to star gaze.

33 Southern Envoy: The Haliburton Highlands and Algonquin Park,
Ontario, Canada. The park straddles a transition between the northern conifers and more southerly hardwoods and has much in common with the Boreal forest.

34 Rapids Trail: A road leading to Oak River. Though the rapids
were gone, the tree name still lingered from times before the river had
been tamed.

35 Lunar cycle: About 29.5 days.

36 Hydrologic cycle.

37 Some lines of evidence Auja provided for a round and spinning earth:

1.   A round earth

   • Taller trees can see further.

   • The sun and the moon are round, why not the earth?

   • The earth sometimes casts a round shadow on the moon.

   • The stars you can see in the night sky change depending where you are.

   • When the Sun is directly overhead in any place, it is not directly overhead somewhere else.

2.   A spinning earth

   • Trees feel it in the winds. Wind never blows straight from areas of high to low pressure because of the deflecting force caused by the rotation of the earth. In the northern hemisphere air masses are deflected to the right, and in the southern hemisphere to the left (Corealis effect).

   Source:
   Firefly Great World Atlas. 2003. Firefly books Ltd.,
      Toronto, Canada.

- A heavy object swinging from a tree vine appears to rotate because the earth rotates beneath it. Trees discovered this almost 400 million years before Foucault's pendulum.

38 Crawler plague: Nuclear Polyhedrosis Virus (NPV) is a naturally occurring pathogen that infects tent caterpillars. Caterpillars ingest the microscopic virus particles while feeding. The virus replicates within the caterpillar's body, turning its insides into a virus 'soup'. The caterpillar breaks open and the soup spills out to contaminate leaves, bark, silk trails etc. The virus takes about nine days to kill.

39 Outbreak: Also known as an epizootic. Epizootics of NPV are often triggered by large host numbers making it easier for the disease to spread. They can cause the collapse of entire tent caterpillar populations.

40 The parasitoid fly, *Leschenaultia exul* (Order: Diptera, Family: Tachinidae) specializes on the eastern and forest tent caterpillars. The insect over winters in a puparium in the soil and emerges in spring. Adults can produce up to 5,000 eggs during their lifetime. Eggs hatch after being eaten by a caterpillar. The maggot feeds inside the host for about fifteen days before chewing its way out and returning to the soil where it remains to start the cycle again the following spring.

Source:

Fitzgerald, T.D. 1995. Tent Caterpillars. Cornell University Press, Ithaca, New York.

41 Trees, unlike humans, were less fussy about the definition of life and considered viruses amongst the kingdoms of the living.

42 Green darner: *Anax junius* (Order: Odonata, Family: Aeshnidae).

43 In other words—there is more than one way to accomplish a task. The expression originates from fur trading times when trees were witness to the slaughter and skinning of fur bearing mammal, like beaver, for their pelts.

44 Half-moon: About two weeks.

45 In fact, including the five pairs of abdominal pro-legs as well as the three pairs of true legs on each crawler, Fur had close to 3,700 legs.

46 This idea was introduced by Benoit Mandelbrot in his 1967 paper in the journal, Science: How Long is the coast of Britain? Statistical Self-Similarity and Fractional Dimension.

If you were to measure a stretch of coast with a metre stick you would get a shorter result than if you used a smaller ruler. In other words, if two creatures—one big and one little—must cross bumpy terrain, then the little creature will have further to go because it takes smaller steps—even if they both start and finish in the same place.

47 Imprinting: A rapid learning process by which a very young animal establishes a behavior pattern of recognition and attraction to another animal of its own kind or to a substitute or an object identified as the parent.

48 Stomata.

49 Mnjikaning: The Mnjikaning fish weirs is a Canadian National Historic Site. Its development began about 5,000 years ago in the narrows between Lake Couchiching and Lake Simcoe, Ontario, and was used to harvest fish by the first peoples of the area. Auja was speaking more generally of modern day Orillia, Ontario.

50 Toronto: Huron (Wendat) for "meeting place".

51 Onitariio: Huron (Wendat) name for Lake Ontario.

52 Auja was referring to the Iroquois Bluff that runs along the current Davenport Road in the city of Toronto, Ontario, Canada. It formed on the shore of the post-glacial Lake Iroquois that once covered all of downtown Toronto below Davenport Rd. Auja might be pleased to know that the bluff is still home to some of the finest stands of Red and White Oak in the city.

Sources:

Environment Canada. Birth of the Great Lakes. Retrieved March 10, 2008, from http://www.on.ec.gc.ca/greatlakes/For_Kids/ The_Great_Lakes/Birth_of_the_Great_ Lakes-WSB2E62708-1_En.htm.

Toronto Green Community & Toronto Field Naturalists. Lost River Walks: Garrison Creek and Nordheimer Reach. Retrieved March 10, 2008, from http://www.lostrivers. ca/GarrisonCreek.htm and http://www.lostrivers. ca/Nordheimer.htm.

53 Wendat: Called the Hurons, by French explorers. They were the union of the Attignawantan, Ataronchronnon, Tohontaenrat and Attigneenongnahac and closest to Auja, the Arendarhonon. The Wendat were the most common peoples in the Southcrop area just prior to the fur trade.

54 Anishinabek: The Ojibwa. These 'first peoples' were originally hunter gathering shield-dwellers to the north of Southcrop Forest prior to the fur trade.

55 The route traveled by Samuel de Champlain, along the St. Lawrence, Ottawa, and Mattawa rivers, then Lake Nippissing, French

River, Georgian Bay, and the Severn River finally reaching the South-crop area in 1615.

56 White Bear waters: Hudson and James Bay—southern home to the polar bear. Auja was referring to the Hudson Bay Company fur trade route through these waters.

57 Small pox.

58 Haudenosaunee: Often referred to as the Iroquois, Iroquois con-federacy, or Longhouse League—comprised of the Seneca, Cayuga, Onondaga, Oneida, Mohawk and Tuscarora.

Sources for endnotes 53-58:

Aboriginal Peoples circa 1630, 1740 and 1823. The Atlas of Canada, Natural Resources Canada.
    Retrieved March 10, 2008, from http://atlas.nrcan.gc.ca/site/english/maps/historical/aboriginalpeoples.

Hunter, A. F. 1909. A History of Simcoe County. Retrieved March 10, 2008, from http://www.waynecook.com/hunter.shtml.

Posts of the Canadian Fur Trade. The Atlas of Canada, Natural Resources Canada.
    Retrieved March 10, 2008, from http://atlas.nrcan.gc.ca/site/english/maps/archives/4thedition/historical/079_80?l=5&r=8&c=8.

The Native Peoples of Simcoe County. 1999. Innisfil Public Library. Retrieved March 10, 2008, from http://www.innisfil.library.on.ca/natives/.

59 The damselfly, Ebony jewel wing, *Calopteryx maculata* (Order: Odonata, Family: Caloperygidae).

60 Order: Diptera, Family: Tachinidae.

61 Gardener Birch's 'garden' also included: strawberry and yarrow, hawkweed and daisy, chicory and vetch, toadflax and trefoil, bugloss and dogbane, loosestrife and fireweed, buttercup and clover, golden-rod and aster, primrose and pearly everlasting.

62 Stigandr: Old Norse name meaning "wanderer".

63 Markland: Old Norse Name for Newfoundland.

64 The Vikings!

65 Possibly the Tunit first peoples.

66 Detritivores and decomposers.

67 Dutch elm disease.

68 Seer Elm was referring to important photoautotrophs that produce organic compounds from carbon dioxide as a carbon source, using sunlight for energy.

69 Carbon Dioxide (CO_2).

70 Sixth element: Carbon. Green plants extract carbon from carbon dioxide via photosynthesis to produce energy rich organic compounds (carbohydrates or sugars) and oxygen. Carbon dioxide + water + sunlight $\rightarrow$ carbohydrates +oxygen. Oxygen (O_2) is used in respiration to extract this energy for use by most life forms.

71 Ecologists refer to this as positive feedback. Any change in the environment that leads to additional and more severe changes in the

same direction. The result of positive feedback is amplification so that small disturbances can lead to drastic changes.

72 The behaviour of the earth system is characterized by critical thresholds (or tipping points) and abrupt changes. Human activities have the potential to switch this system to very different modes of operation that may be less favourable for current life forms, including humans.

For an excellent summary full of ominous examples, see the following source:

Steffen, W., Sanderson, A., Tyson, P.D., Jager, J., Matson, P.A., Moore III, B., Oldfield, F., Richardson, K., Schellnhuber, H.J., Turner, B.L., Wasson, R.J. 2004. Executive Summary. Global Change and the Earth System: A Planet Under Pressure. Sprinner-Verlag, Berlin. Retrieved March 10, 2008, from http://www.igbp.kva.se/documents/IGBP_ExecSummary.pdf.

73 For reasons that are unclear, tent caterpillars do not attack red maple.

Source:

Fitzgerald, T.D. 1995. Tent Caterpillars. Cornell University Press, Ithaca, New York.

74 Bog beacon—a brilliant yellow-headed fungus.

75 Tamaracks are unusual in that they are needle-bearing trees (coniferous) and drop their needles each fall (deciduous).

76 Poplar crust, polypores, golden pholiota.

77 Jelly fungi.

78 Horse hair mushrooms, tan fairy funnel.

79 Blue-green stainer.

80 Little orange log mushroom, yellow fairy cups, orange mycena, tawny pluteus.

81 Farmer Tamarack was referring to the partnership between trees and the mycorrhizae or root mushrooms. These fungi help trees and many other plants acquire essential nutrients and trace elements. Some even help protect trees against disease and soil contaminants. And the trees in turn feed the fungi with the energy rich carbohydrates produced by photosynthesis.

Sources for Endnotes 74,76-81:

Barron, G.L.(1999) Mushrooms of Ontario & Eastern Canada. Lone Pine Publishing, Edmonton, Alberta.

Thorn, R.G. (1991) Mushrooms of Algonquin Provincial Park. Friends of Algonquin Park, Whitney, Ontario.

82 In the form of carbohydrates.

83 A tree shredder, used to clear forested land.

84 Tent caterpillars suffer high mortality during their pupal stage. The juicy pupae are an irresistible delicacy that attracts birds and parasitic wasps and flies.

There were the slender and elegant, Ichneumons (e.g., *Itoplectis conquisitor* in the family, Ichneumonidae, Order, Hymenoptera). They stuck Fur's pupae with their long sharp ovipositors to lay their deadly eggs deep inside.

And of course there was plague. Fur had not emerged clean from blind forest. Many of his crawlers that laid down to rest changed to viral goo—not forest moths.

And finally came the flesh flies, *Sarcophaga aldrichi* (Order: Diptera; Family: Sarcophagidae) to lay their maggots on Fur's cocoons. The maggots chewed through silk and in to the pupae, where they turned their hosts to putrefied soup. Flesh flies like their food just so.

Readers are welcome to send comments and notes on factual errors to: SouthcropForest@sympatico.ca.

CPSIA information can be obtained
at www.ICGtesting.com
Printed in the USA
LVHW03s1433210818
587650LV00001B/173/P

9 780595 495887